# LAKELORE

# ALSO BY ANNA-MARIE McLEMORE

*The Mirror Season*

*Dark and Deepest Red*

*Blanca & Roja*

*Wild Beauty*

*When the Moon Was Ours*

*The Weight of Feathers*

# LAKE LORE

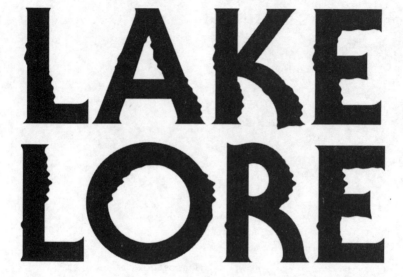

## ANNA-MARIE McLEMORE

FEIWEL AND FRIENDS
NEW YORK

A FEIWEL AND FRIENDS BOOK
An imprint of Macmillan Publishing Group, LLC
120 Broadway, New York, NY 10271
fiercereads.com

Library of Congress Cataloging-in-Publication Data is available.

First edition, 2022
Book design by Liz Dresner
Printed in the United States of America
Feiwel and Friends logo designed by Filomena Tuosto

ISBN 978-1-250-62414-7 (hardcover)
10  9  8  7  6  5  4

*To my mother, who taught me that
the way our brains work holds enough
brilliance to light up worlds*

# LAKELORE

# BASTIÁN

No one believed it when I said I'd seen the world under the lake. But that could have been for a lot of reasons. The first time I found it I was seven, and what adults called *daydreamy*, *lost in thought*, and other words that suggested my imagination might create a whole world out of the lakelore I'd heard growing up.

If I had to guess why no one believed it—other than how I never could find it when I tried to show anyone—it was probably because no one believed it existed anymore. People around here used to. It was once a given that there was a whole world under the lake, that it was half water, half air, that it was as strange and luminous as being inside a sea-foam bubble.

All that was just part of the shared understanding of the lake here, the lakelore. Like fishermen telling how far out storms were by the tint to the sky, or how las viejas measured the seiches so carefully they could predict them like tides.

But as far as I could tell, anyone who took the world under the lake as fact was long gone. The old men gauging the clouds, the old women reading the rise and fall of the water, they were probably the grandchildren and great-grandchildren of anyone who'd believed in the world under the lake.

That part of the lakelore had fallen away, yielding to talk of where opposing winds were likely to make whirlpools or sightings of perch as big as horses. The world under the lake sounded so impossible that no one even made up stories or bragged about it the way they would about seeing ghosts along the western shoreline, or spotting giant prehistoric fish that looked like a cross between dolphins and lizards.

There was no one else here who'd seen the world under the lake, or who even pretended they had.

Then I met Lore.

Not that I knew their name yet.

Not that they did either.

# LORE

The worst mistake I've ever made is bad all on its own, but I never think of it on its own. Some mistakes come in sets, and my worst mistake had a part one that came seven years earlier.

It was on a field trip to a nearby lake, where we were supposed to learn about aquatic and terrestrial biomes. Some of the guys were climbing rocks to see if they could spot high school girls in bikinis on the nearby beach. The rest of us were either studying the craggy shore, looking out for loons (everyone wanted to see their red eyes), or trying to figure out how far we could wander during lunch without the teachers and parent chaperones noticing.

Then there were the few of us clustered close to the volunteer guide, a whipped-cream-haired woman wearing hiking boots and carrying a pocket guide to the local plants and animals. "If the answer's not in here"—she tapped her forehead—"we'll find it in here." She thudded the corner of the book against her palm.

One girl wanted to know if there was really a vanishing lake in Ireland. ("Yes, Loughareema!" the woman said like the words were a song. "One day it's there, the next it's nothing but mud.") A boy asked if lakes had tides like oceans. ("Yes and no," the woman said. "We have seiches, which can look a little like tides, but the moon doesn't set the schedule.")

I asked how much water was in the lake, ready for the thrill of an unfathomably big number.

Then I heard Merritt Harnish's familiar laugh, and my body did what it always did at the sound of Merritt Harnish's laugh. It drew in, like a lake snail curling into its spiraled shell.

I shrank away from the group clustered around the guide.

Later, during lunch, Merritt and his friends were still laughing. "What, so you're smart now?" he asked.

It was, I guess, hilarious to them that someone who could barely read out loud wanted to know things.

He made sure all the adults' backs were turned, and then started mimicking the halting, stuttering noises I made whenever I got to a word I didn't recognize. The heat in my face flared, matches striking against the insides of my cheeks. That fire flew down to my hands so fast I didn't realize I was punching Merritt Harnish in the face until he stumbled back.

The look he got, once he registered what had happened, wasn't the rage I expected. It was almost respect, like he was impressed. He even nodded back at his friends, like maybe he'd just take the hit and we'd all laugh about it.

Then a different laugh, a high, tinkling laugh, sprinkled over us.

Jilly Uhlenbruck, the girl with strawberry-blond hair in strawberry-pink ribbons, wearing strawberry lip gloss, with her perfectly symmetrical dusting of freckles, was watching us. She and her friends, in their rainbow of hair ribbons, perched on the smoothest rocks, lunch bags in their laps.

Jilly's hand was to her mouth. Her glitter nail polish twinkled in the sun, like she was trying to stifle that laugh but couldn't.

Merritt's whole face changed. His next look to me was a glare, as though I'd invited Jilly to watch.

That's when I ran.

That's when Merritt and his friends followed me.

That's when they would have gotten me and probably shoved my face into the dirt if it wasn't for the fever dream that saved me, a boy I'd never seen before, and a world I'm not sure ever really existed.

# BASTIÁN

**T**he first time I saw Lore was near the inlet. At first, I thought the motion rippling the brush was a mule deer, but then I saw someone running. Not running in the laughing way you would with friends—they were alone—or even how you run to get somewhere. They were running in the frantic way of trying to get away from someone, stumbling out of the brush and onto the rocky ground, checking back over their shoulder every few seconds.

I guessed they were about my age. And maybe this is because I'm trans, and always looking out for it, but I got the flicker of recognition that comes with finding someone else like you. A feeling that whatever words this person got assigned at birth maybe didn't fit them either.

It wasn't really any one thing about them. The dark

brown of their hair was in two braids, heavy enough that I could hear them hitting their shoulders as they ran. Their jeans had a rip in the knee that looked recent, not yet frayed. Blood and gravel dusted the edges of the rip, like they'd just fallen.

Their T-shirt was the orange yellow of Mamá's favorite cempaxochitl, the kind of marigold that looks like firewood crumbling into embers. Which wasn't doing this person any favors if they didn't want to be spotted.

None of that told me anything for sure. Gender identity never reduces down that easily anyway. Recognizing someone like you is never as simple as picking things apart to see what they add up to.

They tripped, hard, hands hitting the ground in a way that made me wince.

I went halfway up the path from the inlet, close enough to yell, "You okay?"

They startled so hard that I knew I was right. They were running from someone.

"Do you need help?" I asked.

They looked around for where my voice came from, and found me.

Maybe it was seeing someone else like me, brown and maybe trans, that made me call out, "Come on."

I planned to help them hide out behind the rocks. Then I saw the first flicker of iridescent blue lift off the water. It fluttered through the air, a slice of lake-silver wafting like a leaf. Then another followed it. Then a few more, then a dozen. Then a hundred, each of them like a butterfly with its wings made of water. Then a whole flock of blue-green and silver-blue wings, their backs shining like the surface of the lake.

They spooled away like they always did, showing me the dark underneath the water.

The person I'd just met stared into the shimmering dark. And it took that for me to realize they'd seen it.

The world under the lake had opened for someone besides me.

Maybe it was the wonder in their face. Maybe it was the raw fear. But I led them into the world under the lake, a place I'd never shown anyone because I'd never been able to show anyone.

They looked around and wondered at the coyotes and sharks with eyes that glowed like embers, and the water star grass growing taller than either of us.

They didn't stay long. Just long enough to make sure they'd lost whoever was following them.

I didn't find out their name, or their pronouns for sure, not then. As soon as the world under the lake opened back up to the inlet, they took off, yelling "Thank you" over their shoulder.

Sometimes I do things without thinking, and back then I did that a lot. Talking faster than I was supposed to. Interjecting a random fact about limestone or dragonflies without giving any context. Leaving to do something Mom asked me to do while she was still talking, because I was pretty sure I knew what she wanted from the car, and I was never any good at standing still and listening to directions.

But the other side of that is that sometimes I freeze. When I should do something, I stay still. So many corners of my brain buzz at the same time, a hundred threads of lightning crackling through dry air, that no one thread comes forward. No path or direction makes any more sense than dozens of others, and I do nothing.

So I realized, about a minute too late, that I should have asked where to find them. Or at least called after them to ask their name.

But by the time I thought of that, they were gone.

# LORE

I never told anyone what happened, what I saw.

And Merritt never told anyone about that hit I got in. He'd never admit that a girl had gotten him. Not that I was a girl, but that's how he saw me. That's how everyone saw me back then.

But Merritt shutting up didn't stop Jilly and her friends. So he got a good couple of weeks of *When's your next fight? I want to make sure I get a good seat*, and *You want my little sister to kick your ass next?* And he never forgot it.

He pretended he did. But I saw it in his face, years later.

I wish that had been the last time I fought back, the only time, but it wasn't.

# BASTIÁN

**M**y parents have different memories of what made them take me to Dr. Robins. Mom says it was my changes in speed, the pacing around, climbing things, and then staring out windows, not hearing her when she talked to me. Mamá says she started worrying when I was inconsolable over forgetting a stuffed bear at a park, not because I didn't have the bear anymore, but because I thought the bear would think I didn't love him.

My brother thinks it was the thing with the cat.

I kept ringing the neighbors' doorbell every time their cat was sitting outside like she might want to come in, and then started sobbing about whether the cat was okay when Mamá told me *you have to stop doing this*.

All the restlessness inside me was spilling out, like I was too small to hold it all. If I had to sit still, I bit my nails or pulled at a loose thread on my shirt. Adults kept calling me *daydreamy* and *lost in thought* like they always had, but now they also called me *fidgety*, *a nervous kid*, or they used euphemisms. And I knew what every one of them meant.

*Trouble staying on task* referred to me filling in half a coloring page and then deciding I absolutely had to check on the class fish, right then. *Difficulty listening* meant I might have been listening, but the directions didn't soak into my brain enough for me to do what I was supposed to. *Overly reactive* meant that when I accidentally knocked over a jar of paint or broke a pencil, I treated it as a disaster I had caused, like all the other paint jars and pencils might follow suit and just tip over or snap on their own.

Somewhere between that first appointment and when Dr. Robins explained to me what ADHD was, Antonio sat down with me at the kitchen table on a Sunday. "You having a rough time, little brother?" he asked.

I didn't answer. I kept coloring a drawing, trying not to grip the pencils so hard they'd crack in my hands.

"We're gonna do something together, okay?" Antonio said. "You and me."

That was the afternoon he taught me to make alebrijes, to bend wire into frames, to mold papier-mâché, to let them dry and then paint their bodies.

"Our bisabuelo," Antonio told me as he set out the supplies, ran the water, covered the table, "the family stories say he learned to make alebrijes from Pedro Linares himself, did you know that?"

Everything I knew about alebrijes I knew from Antonio. He crafted whales with magnificent wings. Birds with fins for tails. Snakes that looked like they were trailing ribbons of flame.

"When I don't know what to do with something," Antonio said as he adjusted the curve of a wire, "I do this." He said it as casually as if he were talking to himself.

"If I have a bad day, or a fight with my girlfriend, or I'm frustrated with something at work"—he went on later, the milk of papier-mâché on his fingers—"I just think about it when I'm making alebrijes. For just this little bit, I think about it as much as my brain wants to."

My inexperienced fingers made lumpy, nondescript monsters that looked like rocks with wings, or lopsided fruit with equally lopsided antlers. Not the perfect animals Antonio made, like the one he was working on now, a lizard with fish fins and a flamelike tongue, so it looked like a dragon.

But I watched him, and I listened. My hands bent the wire, held the cold papier-mâché, glided the paintbrush over.

Everything rushed into my head at once. The neighbors' cat. The stuffed bear. How hard it was for me not to interrupt people, not because I didn't care what they were saying, but because I could guess where they were going and was excited about it. How when people got too close to me I wanted to physically shove them away, and it took so much energy not to.

"One thing, okay?" Antonio said.

I looked up at him.

"Just pick one thing that bothers you," he said, "and give it as much space in your brain as it wants, just for now."

I shut my eyes. I tried to let one thing float up from the chaos in my brain.

What I thought of, though, wasn't the cat, or the stuffed bear.

It was Lore. It was how I didn't even know how to look for them. I'd lost them, so now I'd keep being the only person around here who knew the lakelore was true.

"And then," Antonio said a while later, when he was painting the lizard that looked like a dragon, "when I'm done, it's like I can let it go. I got to make it into something, and now it's something outside of me, and it doesn't bother me so much, you know?"

I was painting marigold orange onto the back of an alebrije that looked a little like a mule deer. My hands were so restless that my brush left wispy patterns.

But by the time I was done, my hands were a little

calmer, my brushstrokes a little more even. The beams of light in my brain, the ones always going in different directions, converged on this one small thing, on this brush, on these colors.

I turned the deer in my hands.

Like Antonio, I had made what bothered me into an alebrije.

It was now something outside of me.

So I kept making them. When something I did wrong got stuck in my brain—when I was frustrated, or impatient, or restless—I made an alebrije.

The yellow marmota with sherbet-orange wings was me losing a take-home test.

The teal cat with the grass-green peacock's tail was the panic of realizing I'd messed up a course of antibiotics, because I hadn't learned to keep track of when I ate or when I took pills or even just time itself.

The brown horse with the copper wire tail was my whole body tensing with the effort it took not to kick the guy at school who called me a name I knew the meaning of, but that I also knew I couldn't repeat to any adult.

A butterfly-spider painted as colorful as a soap bubble reminded me of how painfully slowly I had to learn to transition topics in conversations. I had to learn to say things that connected with what everyone else was saying instead of following my brain as it skipped forward, otherwise I'd get looks of *How did you get there?* or *What does that have to do with anything?*

When Dr. Robins asked what I did when I got frustrated or overwhelmed, and I told him about Antonio and the alebrijes, he said, "You have a good brother." He told me the painting and sculpting I was doing helped with *emotional regulation*, that it helped interrupt *cycles of rumination*, terms I was just starting to understand.

There was just one problem.

Within months, the alebrijes crowded every surface in my room. Everywhere I looked, there was a reminder of how many things I worried about, or got fixated on. There was a bat made when Abril frowned and I was convinced she was mad at me and I had done something horrible but couldn't figure out what. There was a squirrel that held my guilt over yelling *I hate this family* to my parents because I was hurt about my abuela's reaction to me changing my name. There was the rounded, porpoiselike body of a vaquita, containing my frustration about the day I mistimed taking my medication, accidentally took it twice, and fell asleep during class.

When I tried to put them away, I felt their agitated buzzing from inside my drawers or under my bed, loud enough that I couldn't sleep. I couldn't throw them away, not when they were the craft my brother had taught me, this art that went back to our great-grandfather. I couldn't give them away; that would be giving someone else things I wanted to forget.

I couldn't ask Antonio what to do either. I imagined him whistling in wonder. *Wow, all of those? That's how often something happens that you need to let go of?*

But I had to do something with them. Their sheer numbers were proof of how often I struggled with the ordinary work of existing in the world.

I did figure it out eventually.

It just cost me the world under the lake.

# LORE

W hat happened?" my parents ask as soon as they see me.

My head feels lined with concrete or brick. My tongue feels dry as masa flour. My mouth wouldn't form the words to explain even if I had them.

"What happened?" They both keep asking, in more urgent pitches, like they're trying to break some part of me open, to make it give up the whole story.

Then I realize what they're staring at.

What they're talking at, what they're trying to make give up the secrets they want, isn't me. They're not looking at my face.

They're looking at the blood on my shirt.

I blurt out, "It's not mine."

As though that makes any of this better.

# BASTIÁN

The path into the world under the lake shivers open, like a whirl of iridescent leaves.

The alebrije I'm holding looks a little like a primeval dolphin, the kind that people sometimes swear they've spotted in the lake. The colors I painted onto the dolphin's back, the greens and blues of the lake itself, are still wet. They gleam in the sun pouring over the inlet.

I set the dolphin down on the lapping water. The teal body stretches and grows until the alebrije looks like some ancient sea dinosaur. Then the alebrije swims down into the world under the lake.

I breathe out, feeling the alebrije carrying off a day I lost worrying about how to talk to my relatives about being on testosterone. It drained away hours and all the energy from my brain. And then I beat myself up for fixating on it (because why just be anxious when you can be anxious about being anxious?).

So I made this alebrije. And as I painted the dolphin's fins, my brain started to unknot. The tension passed from my fingers and into the bristles and paint.

It doesn't mean I'll never feel that anxiety again. I know myself too well to think that. But making the alebrije lets me stop beating myself up about it.

I set down another alebrije, a mint-green fox trailing an emerald-green peacock's tail. This one's for yesterday afternoon, when it got busier in the copy-and-print shop than I've ever seen it. I was holding four different tasks in my head, and three different customers' questions, and when another customer touched my arm, everything flew out of my brain, because that's what happens when someone touches me and I'm not expecting it or don't want it or both. Everything spills out of my brain. My working memory chucks it all into long-term storage, and good luck to me if I want to find any of it anytime soon.

The dolphin and the peacock-tailed fox weave down into the world under the lake, crossing each other's paths as they go. I stand at the edge of the water, watching them vanish.

I might never have figured out what to do with the alebrijes if it wasn't for my ADHD. I'm naturally clumsy, but I particularly excel at dropping things because I forget they're in my hands. One day I was fidgeting with an alebrije at the inlet, and I accidentally dropped it. The raccoon grew, sprouting purple fur. The webbed hands looked real and slick as a salamander's. The alebrije bounded into the dark.

So I brought all my alebrijes to the world under the lake, and the world under the lake brought them to life. They made the world under the lake theirs, taking the shadow boxes inside my brain with them.

At first I thought I could have both, the world under the lake and this way to let the alebrijes go. But the first time an alebrije tried to follow me above the surface, trailing after me like a puppy, I knew it was the last time I would ever go down there.

So I never go farther than where I'm standing now. If I don't want to risk those shadow boxes finding their way back to me, I can't.

# LORE

**M**y parents call it.

"No," I tell them. "We don't have to leave."

I took the suspension. I issued the required apology, teeth gritted. It was received and declared accepted, teeth clenched.

"Why do we have to leave?" I ask.

But they know it's over.

After what I did, and how it happened, it was never not over.

They find a good rate on a rental that's been vacant for months, far enough away to be in a different school district.

When we pack everything up, they act like there is nothing out of the ordinary about this move. Nothing is making us leave. They act as though we all just need a change of scenery.

So I act that way too.

# BASTIÁN

Abril and Vivienne have been nauseatingly cute ever since they admitted they've liked each other since third grade. They hold hands as they go down the sidewalk. The light through the trees casts leaf shadows on their arms.

"Today's the big day, right?" Abril asks me.

"You know I'm not coming back from the first appointment with a deeper voice and facial hair, right?" I ask.

Abril rolls her eyes. "Thanks for clearing that up."

"Hey, you know you have a friend here, right?" Vivienne asks.

I try to parse what she's saying, if this is a *you're not alone* talk. I appreciate the sentiment, but the meaningful way Vivienne's looking at me is making me nervous. Did she mix me up with my brother? The thought of an injection or a blood draw makes Antonio tense in a way that's obvious even if he never says anything about it. Needles have never bothered me. When I was growing up, my parents used to send me along to Antonio's doctors' appointments to distract him with my strings of non sequiturs about oceanic trenches and solar flares.

"She means a fellow nonbinary friend," Abril says. "They're our age. Vivi just met them."

"They seem nice," Vivienne says, which means absolutely nothing because Vivienne thinks everyone's nice unless they prove otherwise. "Their family just rented the apartment above that empty storefront."

"That place that's been vacant forever?" I ask.

"Because it's haunted," Abril says.

"We are not having this conversation again," I say.

"That building is angry," Abril says. "You can just tell."

"That building had termites and dry rot," I say. "It was vacant because they had to fix it."

"That was a while ago," Abril says. "What about since then?"

I look at Vivienne. "Please don't tell me she's convinced you."

"I really don't care," Vivienne says. "Just go say hi to them, okay? You should know each other."

"Because we all rove around in packs?" I ask.

"I mean, don't we?" Abril asks.

She's not wrong. I'm the only one of our friends who's

trans, but we're all queer. Abril, Vivienne, Sloan, Maddie, and I were friends before any of us came out. Most of us found one another with a look across the classroom or playground, half curiosity, half recognition, that look you get when you meet someone and realize you have something in common, whether or not you can name it. Maddie calls it the Queer Bear Stare.

"Because"—Vivienne eyes both of us, her big-sister look—"nothing makes you want to be invisible more than thinking there's no one else around like you. So just go introduce yourself."

I laugh. "Yeah, I'm not doing that."

"Why not?" Vivienne asks.

"Do you introduce yourself to every lesbian who moves here?" I ask.

"Every one I know about, yeah," Vivienne says.

Abril smile-winces. "How do you think we ended up in that book club?"

"I thought you liked Virginia Woolf," Vivienne says.

"That doesn't mean I want to discuss the Clarissa-Sally kiss with little old ladies who know my abuela," Abril says.

Vivienne looks back at me. "Please?" she says. "If you'd just moved here, wouldn't you want to know there's someone else like you around?"

"Wouldn't you want all the friends you could get if you'd just moved into the angry house?" Abril says under her breath.

"Abril," Vivienne says.

"Okay, fine," I say. "I'll do it. Trans unicorns unite." I bow, and then pull out the little notebook I keep in my back pocket.

The weather in my brain today is good. It's blue and misty, like after a soaking rain. I have the reserves to humor my friends.

"It's going in the notebook," Vivienne stage-whispers. "That means they'll actually do it."

That's usually true. In this case, though, I'm lying. But to convince Abril and Vivienne, I need to write it down. Mental notes don't stick in my brain, and they both know it, so this is the fastest way to close this topic.

Vivienne and Abril forget that I don't come off particularly approachable to people I've just met. I have to make an effort not to fill conversational silences that are seconds long but feel three years long to me. And in trying not to do that, I sometimes end up overcompensating, so I come across as withdrawn, uninterested.

I present the open page to Vivienne. Most of my friends at school know I carry little notebooks everywhere—even if they don't know it's to pick up the slack of my working memory—but Vivienne, Abril, Maddie, and Sloan are the only ones I'd ever show them to.

Vivienne grins at the page. I've written *Go be friendly* in my messy but (after a lot of practice) legible handwriting. Even in my own notebooks, I try to keep it legible.

If I don't, and I forget about what I wrote down, I'll come back to it in two days and have no idea what it says. The thought that it was something important and now lost can preoccupy my brain for an entire day.

"Happy?" I ask.

Vivienne grins. "Very."

# LORE

"Aren't you beautiful?" I whisper to the wood I'm sanding. "You're going to be so pretty."

The door to the back workroom creaks open, throwing raw sun over the coating of sawdust on the floor and my jeans.

"I'm officially worried," my dad says.

"Oh, don't even pretend you never talk to the furniture," my mother calls on her way up to the apartment. In this new space, we all have to get used to how sound does and does not carry between the shop on the ground floor and the apartment upstairs.

I go at another patch. "Who decided to throw paint over this anyway?" I brush away the dust. "The wood's beautiful."

My dad dabs at an imaginary tear and sniffs. "I've

never been prouder." A phone rings, and he turns toward the front room.

Summer's always busy. Everyone gets around to things they pushed aside the rest of the year, including getting old furniture fixed up. My parents' reputation for being good and being fast keeps them in business. And ever since they taught me some of the basics—the right way to sand, how to repair a haze or blush on a finish—I've helped them with the fast part. (Case in point, the 150 midcentury chairs we're restoring in time for a wedding next month, a job that will help pay for the move.)

The next time I look up, my mother's in the doorway. "How long have you been working?" she asks.

"I don't know," I say. "A couple hours?"

"Liar," my mom says.

I work on a corner with a patch of paint that won't budge. I'm the reason we had to pack up not just our house, but my parents' whole business. I'm the reason we left the city they lived in since before I was born. And I want my parents to say this, but they won't. So all I can do is sand and paint and oil, and hope it all eventually outweighs what got us here.

My mom twirls her recently-highlighted-at-home hair into a bun.

"Don't panic when you see the calendar, okay?" she asks.

"Starting like that is a great way to get me to panic," I say.

"But there are kittens," she says. It's her usual refrain when there's something on the family calendar I'm not going to like. Just like in our old kitchen, a shared wall calendar alerts the three of us to important appointments and helps coordinate use of the car. My mother always chooses an adorable one so that a weekend set aside for accounting or cleaning out cabinets can be offset with *But there are hedgehogs*, or *But there are puppies*.

"Your first session with the learning specialist," my mother says. "Hour and a half. They won't all be that long. Just the first one."

A sarcastic *I can't wait* drifts into my throat. I bite it back. My mom doesn't deserve that. Not when I'm the reason we're in this town and I'm at a new school that *strongly recommends* I meet with a learning specialist.

"Okay," I say. "When is it?"

"Today," she says.

"Today?" I stop sanding. "Why didn't you tell me earlier?"

She shrugs. "I didn't want you to be nervous."

"What if I couldn't go?" I ask.

"Oh, I'm sorry," she says. "You have big exciting plans?"

"I could," I say. "I already made two friends."

"Dolly Purrton and Catsy Cline don't count."

"Not our neighbors' cats," I say. "I just met two of my future classmates."

"Your appointment's at four." She hands me a piece of paper.

I take it. It has three lines of my mother's handwriting. Bus numbers. Directions. Times. My mother and I are both dyslexic, so how is her handwriting always neater than mine?

"Do you remember this place?" my mother asks, as casually as if musing about making aguas frescas.

"What place?" I ask. I didn't come with them to look for a place to rent, so I didn't see this one until we moved in.

"You've been to the lake here before," she says.

I look toward the front window as though I can see the water from here. "When?"

She shrugs. "It was a while ago."

A noise, a voice, shivers from a wall. It sounds like a laugh. And a creepy one, high and fake. It's a horror movie laugh, the kind you'd hear from a ghost girl.

My mom pins her bun in place with a few old detailing brushes. "What's that face?"

"Didn't you hear that?" I ask.

My mom stares at me. "Hear what?"

# BASTIÁN

**M**om flips open a magazine. "Oh good, Christmas cookie recipes."

I give her the laugh she's trying to get out of me. One of the small joys Mom finds in waiting rooms is how out of season the magazines are.

But my laugh comes out broken and nervous, and she hears it. She must, because she asks, "You doing okay?"

I nod. She probably thinks I'm nervous about my first shot, but I'm not. A nurse who's done this a thousand times will do the injection. And when I think about what's going to go into my body, I feel every cell in me shifting into place. It's like the glitter in the glitter jars I make, wafting through the water and settling at the bottom.

What I'm nervous for is my second shot, the first one I'll do at home. It'll require me to follow directions that, like a lot of directions, are probably simple to almost everyone else but complicated to me.

I run my hand over the sleeve of my jacket. The grain of the wale under my fingers calms me down. The right textures help me hold on to good weather in my brain. It gives me space to remind myself that the nurse will teach me how to do this. She won't send me home expecting me to just know.

I wait for them to call my name. Last, not first. I've always appreciated that, since a lot of us don't have legal names that match us. I'm lucky enough to be done with that part, now legally Sebastián Mario Silvano (I picked the first name with my brother's help; Mom and Mamá picked the middle).

Mom turns the magazine pages. "Your brother wants to know when you're gonna go see him."

"I will." I pick up a science magazine. "I just need to get off work."

"Because the copy-and-print is going to crumble without you?" Mom asks.

"I do have a way with the laminating machine," I say.

Mom gets absorbed enough in instructions for making an ornament wreath that I get out of telling her why I've been so slow in giving Antonio dates. I don't want to tell her the truth, that I'm stalling on telling him about the testosterone.

I want to tell him. Antonio taught me to form wings on the back of an axolotl, or fins on a jaguar, and then paint them in the same brilliant colors our great-grandfather used. He showed me how to turns things my brain gets stuck on into alebrijes.

But he's also the Antonio with a wife and two dogs and a house they just moved into. I am barely more than half his age, sixteen to his thirty-one, and I am about to deep dive into a world he's half a lifetime away from. New facial hair and sometimes-painful growth spurts and probably worsening acne and awkward voice cracks.

A shine on the floor pulls my attention down. It takes me a second to register what the gloss over the carpet is. It's a thin layer of water, like the lake lapping at the pebbled shoreline.

Another skims in over it. Veils of water overlap like translucent fabric. Where the light through the waiting room window hits, it catches the glitter of silt.

I look at my mom, but she's still flipping through the magazine.

"Mom?" I say.

She makes a *hmm* noise under her breath to tell me she heard me, to ask what I want.

I look at the few other people in the waiting room, but no one else notices. One man crosses and uncrosses his legs, which sends ripples through the water out from his shoes.

A door opens.

"Silvano," a nurse in pastel scrubs says.

I stand up, the automatic reflex of hearing my name called in here. I brace for my shoes to squish against the soaked carpet, but nothing.

I look down. The carpet, dulled by sun and age, has the fuzzy look of being dry again. Dust motes wink in the light through the window.

Mom watches me hesitate. "You want me to come in with you?"

"No," I say. "I'm okay."

She tips her head toward the door "Adelante."

I walk toward the door where the nurse is waiting, and the world feels hazy around the edges, like it does when you're waking up.

The nurse goes through the standard checks, and I keep looking for the shine of water on the floor.

By the time we're in the exam room, and she's talking me through how to do an injection, I've convinced myself that it was a trick of the light. Or that nerves made me carry a piece of the world under the lake here with me. Maybe it's my brain's version of the turtle stuffed animal I took everywhere as a little kid.

*Watch what she's doing*, I tell myself. *Listen to the words she's saying. You need to know this.*

But that's the thing about my brain. I can watch. I can listen. That doesn't mean I get it. I can pay all the attention I have and still not understand.

As the nurse gets to the part about drawing from the vial, spines of color appear behind her. Spindly plants like branching coral sprout from the supply drawers. The thick fluid in the vial she's holding turns a deep blue, the color a child might use to fill in an ocean.

As she keeps talking, my mouth stays half-open, and I can't figure out how to either close it or ask *do you see that?*

The nurse keeps going with the brisk, precise instructions of someone who's done an uncountable number of injections. And because I didn't absorb the first part of the directions, I'm already behind, so I can't follow what she's saying now.

The deep blue pulls into the barrel of the syringe, and it looks like the bright cobalt of the sky just before it gets dark.

The nurse keeps talking, and the spindly branches reach out like the purple fingers of Mexican sage. They grow toward the fluorescent lights like they're looking for the sun.

The world under the lake followed me here. Did I bring part of it with me by mistake? Did some of it stick to me the last time I brought an alebrije to the inlet?

"You still with me?" the nurse asks.

I shake my head, an involuntary snapping back to attention. "What?"

My eyes go past her, but the green and red of the coral has vanished. The fluid in the syringe fades to almost clear again.

The nurse studies my face. "It's really not as hard as it seems," she says. "You'll get it in two seconds. Is there any part you want me to go over again?"

Roughly all of it. I just missed everything she said. So my brain wants me to ask, *Can you say all of that again?* But I'm used to saying I understand things when I don't. I've gotten better about asking questions, saying I need something explained again. But when I panic, it's an impulse my tongue still has muscle memory for. I push away help as hard as I need it. The shame of how little I comprehend something makes me blurt out the opposite. So before I can think about the actual consequences of this lie, I hear myself saying, "No. I got it."

I'm still looking for those branches of color when I realize the nurse just said something else.

"Sorry, what?" I ask.

"You ready?" she asks, and by the way she's holding the syringe I know she's talking about the injection.

"Yeah," I say. "I'm ready."

The needle goes in. The testosterone goes in. I breathe out. It's the same kind of deep, involuntary breath that still happens when people call me a boy and use the right pronouns. It's the calm of something being right.

The slight chill of the testosterone going into my thigh muscle flashes that deep blue through my brain.

"You're a steady one, aren't you?" the nurse says, the hint of some kind of Midwestern accent on the *you*.

"What do you mean?" I ask.

"You seemed all kinds of jumpy when you walked in here," she says. "But I put the needle in and you didn't even flinch." She puts the syringe in the sharps container. "You'll be just fine doing these at home."

She hands me a lot of paper, including a set of instruction sheets with grayscale copies of photos, written paragraphs alongside them. Which would be great except that I know what happens with my brain and complicated directions. As soon as I understand one step, I lose the rest, or how they all go in sequence. The frustration of this will take up all available space in my brain, and the directions will look even more incomprehensible than they did when I started.

These might as well be instructions on building a Mars rover.

She leads me back toward the waiting room. I'm caught between how calm my body feels from the injection itself, from the testosterone finding its way into my cells, and the flinch of wondering if I'm about to see veils of water crossing the waiting room floor. But it's the same patterned carpet.

Maybe this was something I needed to do so badly that the world under the lake followed my anxious heart here. Now that it's done, the world under the lake has pulled back beneath the water.

Mom looks up from a different magazine. "Everything go okay?"

I turn the watchband on my wrist, but then stop myself. Mom knows I do that when I'm nervous.

I want to tell her the truth. *Yeah, it went great. But I don't know how to do the next one.*

Except if I tell her that, she'll say something to someone, ask for them to talk me through it again. And that's going against the current of how I've lived with ADHD, trying to make it small enough that it doesn't inconvenience anyone.

Over years of adapting to living with my own brain, I've perfected a nod meant to convey everything from *yes, I absolutely understood all that* to *of course, I'm fine, definitely not overstimulated/overwhelmed/wishing I could hide under a piece of furniture.*

And it's so convincing that even when I use it on Mom, she believes it.

# LORE

I have no place calling anyone's laugh creepy when my mom, my dad, and I all have the kind of obnoxious laughs that sound a little like farm animals.

But something about that laugh got to me, like I was hearing it through water.

In my room, I line up tiny quarter pints with their name labels. Apricot Sherbet. Hillside Clover. Strawberry Milk.

I try to remember if we came here for vacation. But my parents aren't ones for normal vacations. I grew up on road trips to see things like a Stonehenge replica made of cars (my mom's pick), a giant sculpture of a roadrunner (my dad's), banded rock formations that look painted like rainbows (me). I'm pretty sure my mom was talking about someone's wedding. I've been in three of them, a flower girl in two, a ring bearer in another.

I'm still trying to picture which wedding—which one smelled like the soft green dust of the live oaks here?—as I sort laundry.

I grab an armful of towels and open the washer.

A blue glow makes me jump back.

Streaks of light turn against a blue-black darkness as deep as an ocean.

I blink into the washer.

Those trails of light look like constellations in a slow spin cycle, or cars' lights in a long-exposure photo.

What makes me stare isn't the strangeness of it.

It's the familiarity. The particular way the brightness lies against the dark pulls up a memory, like something hauled up from underwater.

"I thought I heard you in here."

At the sound of my mother's voice, I slam the washer shut.

My mother comes into the hall, carrying a handful of dish towels. When she reaches for the washer door, I brace for her to jump back, to see what I've just seen. A tangle of stars against dark water.

But when she opens it, there's nothing inside but the metal drum of the washer.

She adds the dish towels, and then goes toward the stairs.

I listen to the whirring of the washer, blinking away the points of light I can still see.

That searing brightness against the smooth, perfect dark stirs something, like silt kicking up, catching the light.

"Mom?" I say.

She stops and looks back down the hall.

"Did I"—I start out slowly—"did I come here on a field trip?"

She nods. "You were nine, I think?"

She probably assumes that nothing worth remembering happened on that field trip.

Because I never told her any of it.

# BASTIÁN

The second we're back at home, I tell Mom I have to stop by work, saying *I feel fine, really.*

But instead, I go down to the craggy inlet no one ever sees unless they're hiking by it.

I pass by the old sign that used to say LAKELORE, the wood so weathered that the letters are barely visible now. All on its own, the one word looks lost, so you can't even tell what it's doing there. But there used to be a lot more to it than that. Below that one plank, there was a whole placard, a map lettered with little pieces of old lake folklore. The rumored sightings of ancient dolphins. Giant bubbles floating up from the lake floor, holding curled ribbons of seaweed. There was supposedly even a reference to the world under the lake.

But this was a long time ago. By the time I was born,

storms had broken the brittle wood into pieces. By the time I was five, wind and sheets of rain had carried the splinters away, and all that was left was LAKELORE, that one plank thick and heavy enough to stay.

There's a spare beauty in the thin tree cover and low scrub that can withstand the wind out here, the alternating cold and hot. The rough grass looks like water rippling. Little bits of quartz sparkle in the rocks. But right now, I'm not looking at any of that. Right now, I'm standing at the edge of the water, thin sheets of it lapping over the pebbled floor.

I wait for the edges of the lake to turn into leaves of water, spooling away to show the dark underneath. I wait for those silver and blue-green leaves to lift off and swarm around me, painting over the sky. I wait for the world under the lake to open, so I can look for any sign that something's off, for any reason those threads of lake magic followed me above the surface.

I'm staring so hard at the lake that I don't notice the water around where I'm standing. I don't realize it's flooding into the inlet until it soaks my shoes and the hems of my pants.

# LORE

As I walk, the landscape comes forward a little at a time. First the fog, settling low. Then the edges of the rocks, gray as a moon.

The stretch of the lake with pale silt beaches, the ones that draw tourists, that seems like a different planet from where I am now. This is part of the shoreline where the houses get far apart and the land gets hilly.

This is the rocky stretch I remember. There's not a lot filling out the land here, no thick green, nothing blooming except sprays of wildflowers. The trees grow low, wind-bent from how exposed this side of the lake is. The brush and sage paint the hills soft brown and faded olive.

When I find the sign, I know where I am for sure. It's

not much more than a splintered board on a post. But I can make out the shadow of blue lettering. LAKELORE.

My fingers graze the worn wood, and it sends a shiver of recognition through me. It charges the ends of my hair and the crescent moons of my fingernails.

This sign gave me my name. After I left that strange world underneath the water, and the boy who led me into it, I saw these letters. I'd been looking for my name for months. The name I'd been given when I was born had a kind of weight I couldn't carry. It was so distinctly feminine I didn't know how to hold it up.

I brush off the last half of the word on the sign, the echo of the letters almost clear. *Lore*. The first time I saw it, I couldn't parse the whole word, because I'd never seen the whole word before. But when I saw this second half of the word, I knew it was mine. Those four letters emerged from the middle of the name I'd been given at birth, like a constellation out of a cluster of stars. When I told my parents, they smiled like it was obvious, like they couldn't believe we'd missed it.

*Of course*, my mother said.

*That's it*, my father said.

Under the cloud cover, the rocks along the lake look pale gray. The spray laps at them and deepens them to slate. It's not raining here, not yet, but a storm over the lake is throwing sheets of it against the rocks.

I'm wondering how stable a particular ledge is, how close I can get, and if I'll find pieces of water lifting off the lake. Or if I'll find the world underneath that gave me somewhere to hide.

Instead, I see someone down there, trying to scramble up the side of the inlet as the water comes in, and the rocks and wet silt give out.

# BASTIÁN

There's a reason I don't come to the inlet during storms. The ground goes soft. The rocks get harder to climb.

But the storm over the lake is nowhere close. It's still far on the horizon. The lightning looks as small as filaments of copper wire.

The water rushing in right now, that's something else. I know it as soon as I feel it. I know it even before I notice the deep blue and orange of branching plants, the kind I've only ever seen in the world under the lake until today. They sprout between the rocks and up through the rough ground. They mirror the shape of the lightning across the lake.

This isn't the seiches either. The lake's version of tides are gradual, gentle, not rushing and fast like this.

When I try to get up the side of the inlet, I can't get a good grip. Even if I could, the rocks are sliding.

A voice calls from above me.

"Hey, do you need help?"

I look up.

I can't see their features, just dark hair getting in their face, the sweatshirt, the hand they're reaching down as they say, "Grab my forearm."

"What?" I call over the rush of water.

"If you don't want to pull me down with you," they say, "then don't grab my hand, grab on to my forearm."

I hesitate. I don't know this person, and I have no faith that they're steady enough, no matter what part of their arm I grab. Vivienne and Abril have repeatedly demonstrated the physics of this trying to help each other out of a pool, laughing as they both tumble back in. No one ever realizes just how much you have to anchor yourself to pull anyone else out of anything.

Another sheet of water comes in. This one gets up to my waist. Distant lightning cuts the sky into pieces.

A hand reaches down and grabs my arm just below my elbow. I grab their arm back. They're stronger than I expect, pulling me up enough that I can get myself up over the shifting rocks.

"You okay?" they ask, both of us kneeling on the ground above the inlet.

I press the heels of my wet hands into the dirt. I wait

for my breathing to slow and my heart rate to come down. All the things I've been taught to do since I was a kid.

I get my first good look at this person. My brain starts on the kind of fast inventory I've learned to do in a world that often doesn't like that I'm brown and trans. It's a quick, involuntary gauging of whether the person across from me may or may not like that I'm brown and trans.

The features let me breathe a little slower. Dark brown eyes. Black hair. Hands and face a brown that's somewhere between mine and my brother's.

Then I start to wonder if this person is like me in more ways than that. Their voice is low in a way that sounds like they're putting effort in. The jeans and sweatshirt are loose. The smudged eyeliner is the same green as the leaves out here. The hair's stuffed under a beanie, some of it fluffed out in front to look like a boy's haircut. I used to do that before I cut my hair the same way Antonio does.

But my sense of recognition goes past that, like this is someone I've met before. It's not just about them being brown or maybe trans.

The panic of not remembering someone's name when I really should rears up in me. Church? A friend's cousin? Someone at the school where my sister-in-law works? How many times have I met this person, and how upset will they be that I can't place them? What was I distracted by when I met them? What file did my working memory throw their name and the context into when it had to make room for something else?

"Do I know you?" I ask as we both get to our feet and brush the dirt off our knees.

They look a little panicked, and I realize that how raw my voice is right now made that sound like an accusation. It happens sometimes, even with all the practice I've put in. I talk louder than I mean to. My tone is off, and jarring to other people.

Before I can correct and soften with something like *I mean, do you go to school here?* they say, "Yeah. I'm Lore." Then Lore adds, "They/them."

The name shivers through me, and I almost get all the way there. I almost know as I say back, like I've said so many times, "Bastián, they/them."

Because my brain tends to take in too much at once, it takes me a few seconds to understand what's happening. The shifts in light and color rush in so fast I can't process them.

But in the space between registering Lore's name and me getting all the way to knowing who they are, I realize that the world around us is going dark.

# LORE

I know I look different than I did then. I turned out wide hipped and a height that's neither tall nor short. Back then I was both skinny and a head below most of my classmates. My face looked too small for my not-small features, my mouth too cramped for my teeth. I look different enough now—*settled into yourself,* my mother calls it—that relatives I haven't seen for years and then meet again at weddings or funerals don't place me right away.

So I don't expect Bastián to place me.

But they do. And now I have a name to go with them.

"Hi," I say, the syllable laced with a nervous laugh. I instantly wonder why I thought that the right response. *Hi,* like we're just running into each other.

A blur of blue rushes at us. Bastián pulls me out of the way. I feel the motion of their body, them sweeping me into the arc of their path.

A second later, I'm against them, my shirt against their sweatshirt.

"You okay?" Bastián asks.

We're close enough that our breathing brushes against each other's hair. So it takes me a second to say, "Yeah. I'm good."

Bastián lets go and pulls back. "Sorry."

I look up, and track that rush of blue.

First I take in what it is as it crosses the sky, a spotted fish with a feathered tail that looks blade sharp. Then I take in that the sky is no longer daylight-gray, but purple, dark as the rind of an eggplant.

Ocean plants twist up toward that sky. A starfish with blue swallowtail wings rustles the stalks. The sky ripples with threads of light like sun bowing on the bottom of a pool.

"Are we . . ." I don't finish the thought. It trails off, following the fish swimming into the distance.

I look for what I saw the last time, the flickering of blue, the path between the place underneath the water and the surface, the one Bastián led me down and that I followed back toward the inlet.

But I don't see it.

"How do we get back?" I ask.

Bastián stares into the sky, dread tinting their expression.

The water grass reaches out toward us, stirred like a current's going through it.

"Bastián?" I say. "How do we get back?"

Bastián shakes their head. "We're not under the lake."

As soon as they say it, I see it. I recognize the features around us. Everything is still here, but altered. The rocks have turned deep green and blue, the nearby brush to thickets of pondweed. The hills now look like the contours of a lake bed.

We're not where Bastián led me that day.

We're in a different version of where we were a minute ago.

# BASTIÁN

Lore came back.

The one other person I know of who's seen the world under the lake came back.

"What are you doing here?" I ask. And again it sounds harsh, like I often sound when I'm rushing to ask a question I really want the answer to. And if I can tell I sound harsh, it's really bad, because half the time, I don't know how I come across. Mom will tell me I seem sarcastic when I'm not. Vivienne will worry that I'm upset or agitated when I'm just excited about something.

I'm still trying to gauge how I come across to Lore right now. Part of me thinks if I say the wrong thing, or say it in the wrong way, Lore will just vanish.

"I just moved . . ." Lore breathes the beginning of a word I'm guessing is *here*, then stops.

Lore looks around at the water thyme rippling where the brush used to be. "Who are you?"

I have no idea how to answer that. Who I am now is not who I was when I brought Lore into the world under the lake. I don't even go into the world under the lake anymore.

"Did you know there's a collective noun for a group of polar bears?" Lore asks.

I shudder out of what I was thinking. "What?"

"A group of polar bears," Lore says. "It's called an aurora."

"What are you talking about?" I ask.

"Sorry," Lore says. "You seem tense. I thought you could use a piece of trivia."

I let out a laugh that surprises me more than it seems to surprise Lore. *You seem tense.* I am past tense. We are in a corner of the shoreline that looks like it's been filtered through the lake. And as far as I can tell, we're alone. There are no tiny figures down the shoreline. The boats out on the lake bob on the ink blue of the water, unattended.

Lore's focus stays at the dark ground where the dirt path just was. They watch filmy layers of deep-blue water cross back and forth.

"What?" I ask.

"It's going out," Lore says.

"What is?" I ask.

"The tide," Lore says. "Look."

"There are no tides," I say. "This is a lake. The closest we have are called seiches, and they're different from tides."

Lore turns that stare on me.

"Sorry," I say. "You seemed tense. I thought you could use some trivia."

Lore laughs. "Ten points." They tilt their head at the water skimming over the ground. "Really, though. Look."

I watch, until I see what Lore's seeing.

Those layers of water are gradually receding toward the hills. It's so slight I wouldn't be able to stay still long enough to notice if Lore hadn't pointed it out.

"If the tide—sorry, seiche—is going out," Lore says, "where's it going?"

I shake my head. "No idea."

A second later, Lore is trailing the water toward the ghostly versions of the olive trees.

"Lore." I go after them. "Wait."

Their next step takes them into water deep enough that it's up to their waist.

"Lore," I call out again, louder this time, as I run forward.

The sky flashes to pale gray. Then it settles into the dulled silver it was before. The rocks and hills fade back to their soft grays and browns. The dark silhouettes of trees fill out with olive leaves.

Lore's now at the edge of the brush, jeans soaked, but

standing on dry ground. They're breathing hard, pupils pinned small from the sudden light.

How still they're staying lets me notice the faint wisps of color vanishing off Lore. They're thin and delicate as cobwebs, the bright green of algae, as though the world under the lake has left barely visible threads on Lore.

But I can't tell if it just happened, or if it happened seven years ago.

Lore's glance catches on my wrist. They give my watch a weird look. No one our age wears watches, and I know that. But I've also noticed that wearing a man's watch signals something to people looking at me that they don't even register. It makes it more likely that they'll call me *him* instead of *her*, and while *him* might not be quite right, it's a whole sky closer to right than *her*. That's worth my friends telling me that an analog watch makes me look *about a thousand years old*.

"Please tell me that's not really the time," Lore says.

"Usually about ten to fifteen minutes ahead," I say. "But yeah."

Lore swears under their breath. "I'm late."

I may not always know what to do, especially when I'm knocked off-balance. But I'm not making the same mistake again.

"How do I find you?" I ask, at the same time Lore asks the same thing.

We trade awkward laughs.

There's a bristling energy around Lore, and I know they're ready to run. They're not sticking around for an address or phone number.

"There's a copy place here," I say. "It's the only one. I'm there starting"—I check my watch again, because there's enough in my head right now that I've already forgotten the time—"roughly now until closing."

"Okay," Lore says. "Thanks."

Then they're gone.

# LORE

**E**ven running, I miss my bus, and I have to wait for the next one.

Waiting for the next one makes me mythologically late for one of the most important appointments of my life.

I clatter into the waiting room, and a minute later a door opens.

"Lore Garcia?" she asks.

The title *learning specialist* made me expect a woman in a crisply ironed skirt-suit. Not someone in a plaid button-up open over a band tank top.

"Sorry," I say. The sweat on my face makes locks of my hair stick. But I don't take off my hat. On days when I'm a boy or mostly a boy, I never take off my hat unless I have to. "I know I'm late."

"You're more than late," she says. "We'll reschedule."

No. I cannot reschedule. If I reschedule, my parents will hear about it. Best case scenario, they'll think I'm too much of a mess to make anything of my new life here. Worse case, they'll think I don't give a shit.

"Okay." I sink down into one of the waiting room chairs, the woven upholstery gone fuzzy at the edges. "I'll wait."

"I didn't mean today," she says.

"I'll just stay," I say. "In case anyone doesn't show." I try to give her a pleasant, unbothered look that tells her I'm not a pain in the ass, I'm simply persistent.

"It's your day, not mine," she says.

I open my bag and casually take out my summer reading book to show her that I plan, I think ahead, I take homework seriously. All the things I need her to decide about me.

Whether anyone's willing to say it or not, I know she'll give a full report to my new school. And I need that report to be that I'm a promising new student, not a bad bet. I'm already a brown nonbinary kid who just moved to a mostly white town. If the learning specialist gives me anything less than a sparkling review, the teachers will be even more on alert than they already are. A couple of days being late to class, a badly timed laugh, and they'll decide I'm a lost cause, or worse.

Especially if they all know what happened at my last school.

My fingers find where a hardware store receipt is holding my place.

But when I flip the book open, there are no lines of text.

There's a window of the same deep blue darkness I found in the washing machine.

My fingers scramble to turn the pages, but I can't find the edges.

I slam the book shut.

I try again, a random page.

The book still holds that square of blue. It's lit up with bright points, little bits of fluorescent pink and purple and red, like the dots on the *i*'s in neon signs. They swirl around like they're circling a drain.

I press the book shut again, look up, and smile like nothing's wrong, just in case the learning specialist is looking. But she's in her office, one wall of which has a flag that's all sunset colors. I'm pretty sure it's the lesbian flag. It hovers right over a potted fern.

Out of habit, I made a point to hide the pink and blue of the trans flag and the bright bands of the rainbow flag hanging off the canvas strap of my bag. Shoving them into the bag, out of view, is a reflex, something my hands do around new people or in new places.

But now, I fluff the flags out. I'll take anything that

might convince her to fit me in today, up to and including queer family nepotism.

For the next four hours, I take up this corner of the waiting room. I look through old magazines. I use the one all-gender bathroom I find in the basement of this building.

Kids and parents file in and out, and a few students who look college aged or even in grad school. I stay.

I keep checking the time. My fingers wear the upholstery under me even fuzzier as I realize I'm probably going to miss Bastián. But I stay.

I don't know if it's the flags or if I wear her down. But just as the sun is going behind the buildings across the street, her door opens again.

"It's your lucky day," she says.

I stand up, fast, before she can change her mind.

"Don't get too excited," she says. "We can't cover the whole hour and a half right now. But we can at least get started, so come on in."

# BASTIÁN

"You're the only one who can reason with that thing," Trish says as I'm leaving.

"Nathaniel and I have an understanding," I say.

"You named the laminating machine?" Trish asks.

"I did no naming," I say. "We just made introductions." I check the parking lot one more time, looking for Lore.

"You okay?" Trish asks.

Besides worrying that I'll never see Lore again, I'm great.

"I'm fine," I say. "You sure you don't need me to stay?"

"Get out of here," Trish says.

On the walk home, I work on putting some kind of order to my thoughts. I try to figure out what could have pulled the world under the lake above the surface. It can't just be Lore and me meeting again, not with what happened at the clinic.

The weather in my brain is getting hotter and brighter. The cloud-cover thins out. Tourists may like cloudless skies but I don't, especially in my brain. When the weather in my brain feels cloudless, the heat and glare leaves my mood dried out and brittle.

The minute I get home, Mamá calls from the kitchen, "Your brother says if you don't visit him by the end of the month he's coming to get you."

"I know," I call back.

"He wants to make alebrijes with you," Mamá says. "I like that you two do that together. I like that you do things as brothers."

I go to my room, brain spinning back on its previous axis.

I do what I always do. I take this feeling rattling around inside me and I turn it into paint and papier-mâché. I've done it with days when I was so overloaded I wanted to sit in a closet with a glitter jar and not hear anyone's voice. I've done it with times I've said something stupid because I didn't take two seconds to think first. And now I do it with how worried I'm getting about the world under the lake.

I fall into the calming motion of the brushstrokes, the cold milk of the papier-mâché, the whispering of the bristles in paint. It all eases up my fear that maybe I did something stupid without even knowing it, and that's why today happened.

A flash of motion pulls my attention to the window.

Lore is on the sidewalk outside.

I run for the door before Mamá can. When I open the door, Lore is lifting a hand to knock. Their hair sticks out in all directions from under their hat. There's a bloom of color in their face, like they ran here.

"I'm sorry, I'm sorry," Lore says. "I was late getting the bus, so I was late getting back, and I missed you."

I blink at them. "What are you doing here?"

"I ran into your friends," Lore says. "The one with the month name and the one with the Arthurian name."

"Abril and Vivienne?" I ask. I don't often meet people who seem to live at an even higher frequency than I do, but Lore might qualify, at least right now. If I talked as fast as Lore is right now, Mom would pat the air in front of her and say *slow down*.

"Yeah, them," Lore says. "Sorry, sometimes I make mental notes to help me remember names but then I just remember the mental notes and not the names. Anyway, I told them I was looking for you."

"And they gave you my address?" I ask.

"Sorry." Lore takes a step back. "I didn't mean to creep you out."

"You didn't," I say. "My friends and I just need to have a talk about boundaries. Do you want to come in?" As in, into the kitchen or living room, and not my room. Strangers do not see my room.

Lore follows me inside.

"In their defense," Lore says, "I told them we'd met before, and I said I really needed to find you. I think they might have thought I was about to go for the grand declaration of love."

That actually makes me laugh. "Yeah, that sounds like them. They're romantics."

"Got it," Lore says. "Equal parts adorable and sickening."

"Exactly," I say. "You want anything? You look . . ."

"Terrible?" Lore asks. "It's okay. You can say it."

"I was gonna say flushed. Do you want water or something?"

"Who's your friend?" Mamá asks when we come into the kitchen.

Before I can say anything, Lore says, "I'm Lore. They/them." Lore shrugs at the trans and rainbow scarves on their bag. "Walking pride flag."

The quirk of Mamá's smile as she leaves the kitchen means I can predict what she'll say later. *Your new friend's a character.*

Lore watches Mamá go into the living room, then,

with a lowered voice, says, "Have we covered the necessary small talk?"

"What do you mean?" I ask.

"What happened today?" Lore whispers. "How did you do that?"

"You think I did that?" I ask.

"You did it last time," Lore says.

"No," I say. "I brought you into the world under the lake last time. This time, it came to us. I didn't do that. I wouldn't know how to do that."

Lore looks at my hands and then pulls back.

I didn't even realize I rushed out of my room still holding an alebrije, a gold snake with wings.

"Is that"—Lore glances into the living room too, like they're checking that Mamá is absorbed in watching TV, and then back at the winged snake—"that looks like . . ."

"Yeah," I say. "It's an alebrije. But it's not alive yet."

"Yet?" Lore's whisper thins out.

I slow down and remind myself that Lore doesn't know the world under the lake, or how it works.

"What's an alebrije?" Lore asks.

I thud an open palm against my chest. "You wound me."

"Sorry?" Lore says.

"Fastest possible history lesson." I put down the

alebrije and take a glass from the cabinet. "Alebrijes go back to the 1930s, to the Linares family, specifically Pedro Linares. He dreamed alebrijes, and then made them. They're mythical creatures usually made of combinations of features of different animals. Like a frog with bird's feathers, or a snake with dragonfly wings."

"Or a starfish-butterfly," Lore says.

I fill the glass and then hand it to Lore. "My great-grandfather studied how to make them in Mexico City. He made the papier-mâché kind, so that's what we know in our family. Usually they're made of papier-mâché or wood, and then painted."

"And they're alive," Lore says.

"No," I say.

"But you just said—"

"Can you—" Now I'm the one checking the living room, where Mamá is arguing with a game show while sorting the mail. "Alebrijes are not alive. They're art. Usually. But—in the world under the lake, yes, they're alive. But no one else knows about all this, okay?"

I sigh. "Yeah."

"How do you hide all that?" Lore asks.

"I don't," I say. "I never wanted to. I wanted to show it to other people, but I never could. I never found a way into the world under the lake when anyone else was there. Except you."

Lore's eyes flit around the kitchen, like they're trying

to order the information in their brain. Or maybe I'm just seeing that because that's what I'm so often doing, trying to make the chaos inside my head hold still long enough to let me understand it.

"The world under the lake," Lore says. "That's what you call it?"

"I didn't make it up," I say. "That's what they used to call it around here."

"So we're *not* the only ones who've seen it," Lore says.

"Yes and no," I say. "There used to be a lot of stories about it, but not so much anymore. No one around here really thinks it exists. It kind of fell out of the lakelore."

"The what?" Lore asks.

"The lakelore," I say. "It means all the strange things about the lake. Some of it's science, like the seiches. Some of it not so much, like stories about people seeing bright purple fish. Some of it's in between, like theories that the bottom is a lot deeper than everyone thinks, that kind of thing. That's lakelore."

"Oh," Lore says.

I'm wondering if they're thinking of exactly what I'm about to ask.

"While we're on the subject," I say.

"Yes, I got my name off the sign," Lore says. "That day we met."

Did that tie Lore to the lake, the act of finding their name so close to the water? More than close to the water.

They found their name where so many strange things about the lake were once painted on wood, before storms and swells carried the pieces away like the water was taking them back.

"I don't get it," Lore says. "The day we met, you led me under the lake like it was nothing. I kind of wondered if you lived there."

"You thought I lived there?" I ask. I don't mean to laugh, especially when Lore is this worked up, but I can't help it.

"I don't know," Lore says. "I was nine, okay?"

"I don't live there," I say. "I never did. The world under the lake, that's what you saw years ago. The lakebed, underwater plants, sea glass, and yes"—I lower my voice even further—"the alebrijes. But what happened today. I've never seen that. It's like it came above the surface. That's new."

"So what do we do?" Lore asks.

"What do you mean?" I ask.

"I was late to something today that I really needed to not be late to," Lore says. "What do we do to stop this from happening again?"

The instinct from the clinic comes back, the impulse to lie and say I understand something I don't. But there's no faking it here. I can't just nod and say I know how to fix this.

"I don't know," I say.

I tense, ready for Lore's annoyance, or the veiled rage of *What do you mean you don't know?*

But their next look at me is tentative.

"What if I'm the problem?" Lore asks.

"Why would you be the problem?" I ask.

"Think about it," Lore says. "If what happened today didn't happen before I showed up, maybe I'm the problem."

"That's not possible," I say.

"Why not?" Lore asks.

"Because it's not, okay?"

Lore's gaze and mine meet on the alebrije, listing to the side on the counter, leaning on the corner of a wing.

"I will fix this," I say. "Just trust me, okay?"

"Okay." Lore hesitates, licking water off their lips. "Except you're not alone in this."

I think I'm in control of my facial expression until Lore says, "No, don't roll your eyes. I'm not trying to reassure you. I'm literally telling you that you're not alone in this." Lore reaches into their bag, takes out a book, and opens it.

Where a page spread should be is a patch of dark blue, dotted with lights wider than stars, like a ball of Christmas lights.

"Bastián?" Lore says.

"Sorry," I say. "I'm having trouble selecting the right swear word."

Lore closes the book and throws it in their bag. "When I first met you, you helped me, and you didn't ask questions. So if you're asking me to trust you now, I will."

The way their voice trails off implies the rest of the sentence, the unsaid *but* . . .

"Can I ask you something?" I say.

Lore picks up the water glass. "Sure."

"The day we met, what were you running from?" I ask.

Lore finishes the water and puts the glass in the sink. "I promise you, it doesn't matter." They take a pen off the counter. "This is where I live"—they write on the grocery list, an address I place as roughly in the middle of town—"if you get tired of the lone wolf approach." Lore lifts the strap of their bag onto their arm.

"Lore?" I say.

Lore stops in the kitchen doorway.

"If you can," I say, "stay away from the lake, okay?"

Lore laughs. "You think you have to tell me that?"

On the way out, Lore says to Mamá, "Nice to meet you."

I watch Lore from the living room window.

Mamá looks up from the mail, and I'm pretty sure she says, "You like them."

But when I say, as a reflex, "No, I don't," she smirks.

"I said *I* like them." She grins as she puts stamps on envelopes. "But that's good to know."

# BASTIÁN

On the way back to the inlet, I brace for the sky and the whole world to turn again. But it doesn't. And when leaves of silver and green lift off the water, I set the alebrije down.

The snake's body winks gold, and then grows and stretches like a vine. The scales turn iridescent. The wings gleam polished black. The eyes flare like embers. The bright flame of a tongue licks out.

The snake winds across the ground and then vanishes into the dark.

The alebrijes always seem so happy, as though they're surprised and delighted to find themselves alive. You'd never know that they're carrying away all the times I got things wrong, or did things too fast or too slow. They just stream out of sight, like they can't wait for what they'll find under the lake.

Which is why I don't expect the forms drifting out from the dark. They float forward, features coming into focus. A crab with a fan of blue turkey feathers off each claw. A mule deer with a delicate fishtail fanning out behind it.

"No," I say.

I don't yell it. It's not a word of panic, or even protest.

It's a boundary, a line I'm drawing between the world under the lake and the world above the surface. Between the bad days I've let go, and my life now.

If that line needs to be clearer, I can draw it, right now, as cleanly as a length of wire.

"Your world is there," I say. "My world is here."

They hover, the colors at their edges brightening and dulling like I'm seeing them through water.

"Okay?" I say the word with enough certainty that by the time I'm done with it, it's barely a question.

The alebrijes drift back into the dark.

# LORE

*Leave it alone, Lore,* I answer back to my own brain. *Bastián says they'll handle the world under the lake. So let them.*

I focus on wrapping my brain around my life here. I need to build the muscle memory of writing this address instead of my old one. I need to stop mixing up the area code here with the one where we used to live. I need to learn the layout of these rooms so I stop wandering into walls when I get up in the middle of the night.

As I'm unpacking a box, my hands stop on a familiar shirt. The worn cloth is soft under my fingers, the color halfway between orange and butterscotch, a perfect November-leaf shade.

It used to be one of my favorites before I made the stupidest mistake of my life while wearing it. And I could have sworn I already got rid of it. I didn't get rid of the binder I was wearing underneath it, because, one, binders are expensive. Two, once you find one that fits, you wear it out. Three, I wasn't letting that day ruin my binder for me. My shirt? Maybe. But my binder? No.

A sound fills the room. It seeps up from the carpet. A roiling laugh. Not the low, rumbling cackles of Merritt and his friends. This one is different. Higher, and unfamiliar. It's neither my mother's laugh—full and loud, the one I inherited so precisely no one can tell mine from hers—nor the near chirrup of my father's, the one relatives call his *goose laugh*.

This is the laugh I heard through the walls.

The light goes out of the room, the sky outside, the whole world.

# BASTIÁN

Technically, everything's where it belongs. The floor-model stand mixer that Mom negotiated to buy for a heavy discount. The squares of linoleum that have gone sticky from age and changes in temperature. The lemons in the fruit bowl.

But everything's now either darker or neon-sign bright. The stand mixer's body is fluorescent periwinkle, the mixing bowl as glaring as aluminum foil in the sun. The edges between the linoleum squares look like the orange of illuminated circuit wires. The lemons are lit up like bulbs in a lamp. Outside the window is the kind of dark that seems deeper than nighttime, like how I imagine the bottom of the ocean, or the void between galaxies.

The kitchen light casts the green of wet epazote leaves.

Little points of orange and pink circle around the bulb, changing shape. One second their silhouettes look like moths flitting their wings, then tadpoles swimming, then flashes of flame.

"Mamá?" I call out.

No answer.

The mirror in the hallway swirls with spirals of shimmering gold, like minerals stirred up in a pond.

My throat goes dry. "Mom?" I call out.

The front door creaks open.

I take cautious steps toward the sidewalk, now the vivid blue of the sky here in August.

A cloud of color speeds by, a green axolotl with feathery purple gills and markings like a mezquite bug. Another follows it, an iguana with webbed feet and a mane that looks like fire. They blur through the air and disappear down the street.

Once the alebrijes are out of sight, it's so quiet that my own breathing sounds like noise.

The houses have turned brilliant shades of purple and pink and turquoise. The trees are bare of their leaves, boughs dyed the vivid colors of candy. They look like branches of coral reaching up toward the midnight green of the sky. A neighbor's cat, usually a gray tabby, is the teal of a wet agave leaf. His tongue laps out, bubblegum pink against the blue green of his fur. Another cat, magenta as the lipstick Vivienne wore every day in ninth grade, chases him along a fence that's typically pale wood but is now apple red.

A shadow moves under the branching coral.

First I recognize the hair, cut just above the collarbone. Jeans and a sweatshirt hang loose on their body.

"Bastián?" Lore asks.

I knew who I was looking at. I just didn't realize until they spoke that they were really here.

Two more alebrijes fly past. A green dolphin with red spider's legs, and an owl with a curling tail like a blue alligator lizard's.

We pull back toward the sidewalk and watch them vanish into the night.

Did I do this? Could this be because I brought Lore into the world under the lake when we were kids? Did that one impulse, that one badly thought-out decision, get us here?

I look back into the house. A patch of wall no longer looks like a wall, but like a curtain of rippling water. Light glows behind it, pulling into faint shapes.

"Stay here, okay?" I tell Lore.

The closer I get to that patch of wall, the colder the air feels, sharp as the chill off the lake. I slip my hand through. Then the rest of me.

On the other side of the wall, the air doesn't feel like water. It's glaring, piercing light. It's as bright as the sun sharpening the lake surface. I almost make out the luminous silhouettes of alebrijes, but I can't tell for sure. It's so bright I want to hide from it. It's as loud as every corner of my brain talking to me at once.

I pull back toward the wall. But the wall is still rippling like water, so I fall through it.

On the other side, Lore catches my arm. "You okay?"

I get my footing again. I nod. "Thanks."

I try to make out the bright shapes through the translucent patch of wall.

If the alebrijes are coming back above the surface, the worst of me might come back with them.

That cannot happen.

I cannot let that happen.

# LORE

**B**astián's brain is working so hard, I can practically hear a cooling fan trying to lower the core temperature.

"You're panicking," I say.

"I am not," Bastián says. They were fiddling with their watchband a second ago, but now they stop, like they just realized they were doing it.

"Yes, you are." I don't mean to laugh, but it slips out, nervous, in between my words.

"Well, aren't you?" Bastián asks.

"Oh, I am," I say. "But you're the one who knows what you're doing. I don't."

Bastián's quiet.

"Don't you?" I ask.

Bastián continues to be quiet.

"Okay," I say, and I almost sound calm. "So we look for the tide thing again."

"Yeah, how did you figure that out?" Bastián asks.

"I'm as smart in some ways as I am stupid in others," I say.

"What?" Bastián asks.

"Forget it," I say. The joke doesn't work if Bastián doesn't know how my brain works, and anyway, my mother says I have to be careful with the self-deprecating jokes. *Don't call yourself stupid, even if you think you're kidding.* She says I need to value the things I can do, without qualifying them. I may mix up letters, but I can tell exactly what container will fit the leftovers. I may not know what to do with a word I've never seen written out before, but I can keep maps of places in my head (I'd only been to Bastián's house once, and I knew how to find it again, just like with the bus stop).

Two cats leap by, one green as oregano leaves, the other light blue. I think I've seen them, the usual versions of them, and they're gray and white.

"Radioactive cats," I say.

Bastián looks at me. "What?"

"You've never heard of it?" I ask. "But you're an artist."

"No, I'm not," Bastián says.

"What do you call what you do with the alebrijes?" I ask.

"A way to fidget that involves paint?"

The dreamed-up animals Bastián makes are magic even before the world under the lake brings them to life. Don't they know that?

"*Radioactive Cats* was an art installation a long time ago," I say. "There's a really famous photo of it, and when I was little, I couldn't stop looking at it. It's in this book my parents have. I'll show you sometime. Now are you gonna tell me what's going on?"

"Wow, you change subjects faster than I do," Bastián says.

We keep walking, winding closer to the lake. We pass windows that give off every color from bright yellow to deep blue. We search the streets for the shine of a tide going out—or the lake equivalent.

Just when I think Bastián isn't going to answer, they start talking.

"I use the alebrijes to send parts of me into the world under the lake," they say.

I look at them. I want to ask *What are you talking about*, but the silence between us feels thin, fragile as frost on a window. So I leave it.

"I was"—Bastián hesitates—"hard to deal with as a kid. I was difficult."

To a lot of people, I was *hard to deal with as a kid* too. And right now, probably.

"Part of how I got a little easier to deal with was working on the alebrijes," Bastián says. "That became how I processed things. I took things I needed to let go of and put them into the alebrijes. Then I let the alebrijes go, and it was like they were taking those things that happened with them. So I didn't have to carry them around anymore. And you're not listening to me at all, are you?"

"Yes, I am," I say as I bend down to watch a snake wind through the grass of someone's front lawn. The snake is the blue of cotton candy and no bigger than a hair ribbon. The eyes glint like they have facets, and I'm pretty sure this is Bastián's work. I remember the same kind of glint looking out from the dark the first time Bastián brought me into the world under the lake.

"Hi, baby," I say. My voice does the same involuntary pitch it as when I'm examining a beautiful piece I get to work on. "Aren't you pretty?"

The snake slithers closer to me. Her body gleams as she moves.

"I'd stay away if I were you," Bastián says.

"Why? Does she bite?"

"Just don't get close to the alebrijes," Bastián says. "It's not a good idea."

"So you think they have something to do with all this?" I ask.

"Kind of," Bastián says. "It's more what they brought down there with them. What I tried to send into the world under the lake."

"Why?" I ask.

The snake's eyes shine like lit coals. The yellow and orange glimmers in a way that looks hot.

"So have you ever watched water beading together?" Bastián says.

"Yeah," I say.

"And you know how the beads just find each other?" Bastián asks.

I watch the snake take off into the grass. "Yeah."

"It's called cohesion," they say. "The phenomenon of how particles of the same substance stick together."

"Like how queer and trans people seem to find each other," I say.

"Kind of, yeah, same general idea," Bastián says. "Except that's a good thing. What's happening here, I don't think it's a good thing. I'm worried that something is pulling the world under the lake back up here."

"Like what?" I ask.

"That's what I don't know." Bastián hesitates. "Maybe there's something I should have sent into the world under the lake that I didn't."

I stand up from the grass. "You think there are things you want to forget that are pulling back things you already forgot?"

"I didn't forget anything," Bastián says. "It's not like the alebrijes take my memories with them. I still remember everything. Like that one"—Bastián gestures at the last flash of cotton-candy blue—"I made her during a time when I was pretty sure that someone looking at me a certain way meant they hated me. I remember that. It's not like that ever went away. But sending all of that into the world under the lake meant I wasn't so close it."

As we look for the seiche, Bastián's words knock around in me, like something turning over in the dryer.

If the problem started when I moved here, the problem has to have something to do with me. And if Bastián thinks the problem is about letting go of things, then what I did might be pulling the world under the lake above the surface.

By the time we find the seiche, layers of water receding down a street, I know.

The problem doesn't just have something to do with me. The problem *is* me. And maybe if I can do something like what Bastián does with the alebrijes, I can fix this.

# BASTIÁN

"This can't happen," I say.

Shapes float against the dark.

"I mean it," I say. "You can't follow me back here."

The alebrijes twirl forward. I tense, thinking they're going to rush out from the world under the lake and toward the surface.

"If you do," I say, "everything will fall apart for me. Do you get that?"

The quetzals and mule deer pull back. They stay close to the sea glass.

I try to level out my breathing. "Thank you."

# LORE

Y our teachers' notes mention you're good at spelling," Amanda the Learning Specialist says.

I'm shocked there's anything good left to pull
from my file. After what happened, I'd imagined the school
striking out every positive thing any teacher ever said about
me, a correction written underneath each one. *Never mind.
We take it all back. We knew there was something off about Lore
Garcia the whole time.*

Everyone wants to think they see the best in everyone else, but when the bad comes out, they want to pretend that's all they ever saw.

"You were in the school spelling bee," Amanda the
Learning Specialist says.

"Not really," I say. "I didn't get past the first round."

"What happened?" she asks.

"They had us all take written tests to qualify," I say, "And because I knew how to draw words like *gingham* and *chartreuse*, I qualified."

I hope she's writing down *adapts well. Engages thoughtfully with schoolwork.*

"*Gingham* and *chartreuse*, that was just luck." Yeah, bad luck, but I don't say that out loud. "My parents are furniture restorers, so I know fabric words." I shift the bag on my lap, tiny quarter-pint cans bumping against one another. Noble Petal (blush pink) knocks into Dinosaur Kale (deep forest green). "But then the actual spelling bee was oral, not written."

I flinch at the memory of staring blankly into the school auditorium in a way that Merritt Harnish would mimic for years.

I feel the weight of the paint cans on my lap. Every word from Merritt and his friends, every time they looked at me like I was supposed to confirm how hilarious they were, I imagine all of it streaming out of my hands and into these paint colors. I picture all of it leaving my brain and my body and becoming so contained I can release it into the world under the lake.

"So that's what happened," I say. "I'm only good at spelling if it's written down."

Amanda the Learning Specialist looks at me like she expects me to keep talking. So I do.

"I can't really spell out loud because the letters I see

in my head almost never end up being the ones I say out loud," I tell her. "But if I can write them down, that's when the words can be pictures."

"How are they pictures?" Amanda the Learning Specialist asks.

I think for a second. "I guess when I'm writing them down, letters aren't really letters as much as they're curves and lines. That's what makes it more like drawing than spelling. Sometimes I don't write the letters in order either. I start in the middle sometimes, and I keep adding letters until the word looks right. Until it looks like the word I memorized."

Amanda the Learning Specialist nods.

She doesn't write anything down.

Should I not have admitted that?

"I don't do it with every word," I say. "Like with short words, or words I write a lot, my hands get used to them. It's the longer ones or the ones that don't come up a lot where I end up writing the letters out of order. My mom does it too."

My hands go clammy. I'm talking too much. Usually, that helps me win people over. It loosens them up. With people who aren't talkers, it takes the pressure off. With people who are, it gets them started. But in this room, rambling means eventually I'll say something I shouldn't. So I need to just answer her questions, not open myself like a soda can so she can see what fizzes out.

I shift, and the paint cans rattle.

"I'm sorry, I have to ask," Amanda the Learning Specialist says. "What are you holding?"

"Paint samples." I pull one out of the bag and hold it up.

"And you just carry them around like that?" she asks.

"I like them," I say. "They make me happy."

"Why do they make you happy?" Amanda the Learning Specialist asks.

Her expression is so genuinely interested that it makes me nervous.

If I want to put all the parts of my life I don't want into these paint cans, this is the place to do it. This is the room where Amanda the Learning Specialist asks about my trouble with syllable segmentation, phonemic awareness, open and closed syllables. This is where I have to talk about my particular hatred of Dr. Seuss and the nonsense words he puts in his books, because when you're dyslexic, knowing how to read the word *cat* does not necessarily mean you know how to read the word *bat* or *mat* or whatever made-up word rhymes with them.

Everything I have to talk about here can go into these paint cans.

Everything I don't want to talk about can go into these paint cans.

"I guess I love the names," I say. "Amberglass Blush.

Candy Button." I check the labels on the cans I have with me. "Princess Cake. Boudoir Sky. Which is, surprise"—I hold it up so she can see the paint dot—"not blue but purple."

"So I'm guessing you like those paint-chip-card displays in home-improvement stores?" Amanda the Learning Specialist asks.

"Oh yeah," I say. "That's where my parents could always find me when I got away from them. Most of the words I know how to read I learned from my parents and teachers and librarians reading with me. But the rest I probably learned from paint fan decks. When trips to get supplies took a while, my parents used to bribe me with the promise to buy me one of these." I hold up a quarter-pint can, this one with a dot of apricot orange on the top. "I always picked based on the name."

"How are things going with your family now?" Amanda asks.

Except for how I tore down our life in the city they'd lived in for twenty years, they're flawless.

"Good," I say.

"What about friends?" she asks. "You keeping up with anyone from your old school?"

What I don't say, what I want to say: All my friends liked me. And most of them even stuck with me when I came out (and those who didn't, I chose to forget their names). I was the one they asked what shirts to wear on first dates, what were the best grocery stores to buy flowers to bring their mothers after they stayed out too late. But I don't hear from most of them.

Some of them tried. When I didn't answer, they gave up. There has to be a hard dividing line between what happened and my life now.

"Yeah," I say, tensing so the hitch in my stomach won't show up in my voice. "A few of them."

Amanda the Learning Specialist checks the clock and sees—like I've pretended not to have seen for the past ten minutes—that our session's almost over. "Your homework"—she hands me a workbook—"is to start on that. And bring me your favorite book."

"Like for school?" I ask.

"No," she says. "Your favorite book in general. Doesn't have to be for school."

When I pick up my bag, I swear the paint cans are heavier than when we started.

When I get off the bus home, I go to the inlet.

I know I'd told Bastián I'd stay away from the lake. But if there's any chance this might work, I have to try.

In the dusk, the middle of the lake goes midnight blue. At first, I think the shifting color along the rocks is just splashes of water breaking. But as I stand there, shapes come into focus. A leaf of blue lifts off the surface.

Another follows it. Then a few more, then hundreds, each of them like a butterfly made of water.

I remember this, from that day years ago, jewels of water rushing toward us and painting over the sky.

Then I can see the dark landscape of the world under the lake. Stars swim through it like handfuls of glitter in molten glass.

I'm not going in, even if I want to. The world under the lake is somewhere Bastián brought me once. That doesn't make it mine.

I take out the paint cans I brought with me. I open the pale pink, the storm blue, the green as bright as food coloring.

With each one I open, the world under the lake pulls on the paint, strong as the moon's on the ocean. The color drifts toward the dark, spooling out like auroras in a winter sky.

I can almost hear a faint noise going with it, a twinkling sound like water skipping over metal.

A flare of recognition goes through me. It's that laugh coming off the walls at home. But now it's streaming away, trailing after a ribbon of tangerine paint.

Maybe it's not just me who needed to give things up to the world under the lake. Maybe I was supposed to bring that laugh here, to find a path underwater. Maybe I'm making things right with whatever noise and restlessness is haunting where we live.

The sound lilts and skips into the dark.

I stay in exactly that spot until the cans are empty, so clean of paint there's no trace of color.

# BASTIÁN

"We covered the extra blood pressure checks, right?" Dr. Robins asks. "You can do those at Dr. Russell's office. You don't have to come all the way to me."

While I'm on the phone with Dr. Robins, I make an alebrije, a shark with eyes that glint like live ash. The vial of testosterone sits on the corner of my desk, right next to my meds. Easy reach for reference.

"Meds still feeling okay?" Dr. Robins asks.

"Yeah," I tell him, and we talk about my dosage and the timing. ADHD medication helps give me more of a buffer against changes in my brain weather. I used to get startled by a noise and be thrown off for hours. Someone would give me a look that could have meant nothing, and the ground of my thoughts would dry out and crack. That still happens, but it happens less often, and it happens slower.

This morning I missed the time I usually take my meds. I woke up groggy, tired from dreams of the lake flooding onto the shore, the water pulling into the shape of flames and licking across the hills. So I'm back to setting alarms.

"Any side effects I should know about?" Dr. Robins asks.

A note I put on my desk reminds me. I can never remember this stuff in the moment. "There's this occasional twitch in my thigh muscle," I say. "But it doesn't really bother me."

"Let's keep an eye on that," Dr. Robins says. "You feel ready for your next injection?"

What I tell him: "The nurse gave me some practice syringes and told me to rehearse with saline and fruit."

What I don't tell him: I'm still trying to make sense of the directions.

When I get off the phone, I pick up the vial. I shut my eyes, the glass cool against my palm.

If I tell Mom and Mamá that I didn't catch any of the nurse's instructions, they'll remind me that I need to speak up when I don't understand things. And they'll mean well, but it'll be a speech I've heard before and a bunch of *I know, I know* that they've heard from me. Mom and Mamá forget sometimes that it's not that I don't know what to do. It's how much my brain resists remembering what I need to do in the moment, and then actually doing it. And explaining that is almost as frustrating as reading directions.

A noise like rushing water comes from outside. Not the hollow echo of someone running a sink or taking a shower, but the force of water hitting the ground. It sounds like hard rain, or the crackling of embers.

When I open my eyes, I almost drop the vial. The fluid inside is now the same deep, illuminated blue it turned in the clinic.

Spills of color drift through my room. Cobalt-glass blue and the red of chili powder and the green of wet grass spread across the air. They thin out and go translucent, like drops of food coloring in water.

I set the vial down and go to the window.

Water skims over the street. But it's not going out like a tide. The water's rising. It's rushing in hard enough for the surface to foam. Strands of lake kelp tumble underneath.

My breath buckles and halts, like those bright green ribbons snapping in the current.

I call Mom's and Mamá's names, just in case I'm wrong, just in case I'm not alone in this world-under-the-lake version of our house.

No one answers.

Sometimes how fast I think makes me slow to make decisions. It means I take in so much information I can't put it in any kind of workable order. So in those rare moments when I know exactly what to do—not because I'm letting my fear or my first impulse decide, but because I can feel in to my cells—I'm sure.

I check the address Lore wrote down, and I run.

# LORE

I scrub my hands at the sink, my clothes smelling of varnish and sawdust. As the water spins down the drain, it throws off little arcs of color, like sun through prisms. Or the swirl on the surface of a bubble.

I look up.

Everything is brighter. The bathroom counter is the color of lemon meringue pie. The towels on the rack, usually faded orange, glow as bright as bell peppers.

"Mom?" I call out.

When I step into the hall, the carpet under my feet is the color and texture of pincushion moss.

I take a few more steps. "Dad?"

When a sound comes back, my heart jumps, thinking my parents are here.

But in the next split second, the sound gets clear enough for me to know it's not a voice.

It's the tumbling, foaming noise of rushing water.

It floods into the hallway, rising, throwing cords of green and blue and rust-colored kelp at my legs. As I go for the stairs, the ribbons grab at my calves, and I have to fight as hard as if I'm running through mud.

The current pours down the stairs into the shop, turning the wood steps into a waterfall. I cling to the railing so the force doesn't knock me over.

The water on the ground floor is high enough that the furniture-in-progress is floating. A cabinet that's usually a dark, rich wood is now a bright red, and it knocks into a desk that's usually a blond finish but is now a glaring blue. A yellow end table collides with a coffee table that's suddenly the purple of violet petals. They all clatter against one another. Inside the noise of them knocking together, another sound emerges, one that's bristled against the back of my neck for half my life.

It comes with the words *sound it out*, said in a repeating chorus. These are boys who like seeing the anger surge in me, the way my knuckles go tense as I hold it back. They know that I know I have to cram all that rage back inside me, because I am brown, and queer, and nonbinary, and I cannot get away with fighting.

That chorus changes shape. It coils in and billows out and twists into that laugh coming off the walls. It's back, and it's louder, singeing the edges of my thoughts so nothing else gets in. It's a flame sealing off the ends of a rope, leaving it glassy, impenetrable.

I hear my name in an unfamiliar boy's voice, and I pull back.

I can't see them, any of the boys whose voices are finding me again. But they're echoing off the walls.

Kelp and branches weave up from the floor. The kelp grabs at my legs. I stumble against the branches, and they're as hard as the boughs of a full-grown tree.

"Lore." The unfamiliar boy's voice calls my name again.

I turn. A forest-green table rides the current and catches me in the side. It hits hard enough to take the wind out of me, and I fall back on it. The kelp grows thicker in the water, and the water twirls around it in eddies and tiny whirlpools. The branches climb up toward the ceiling.

But I don't move. I don't have enough air back in my lungs to move.

A boy's shadow falls over me. This boy will draw back his fist, and I will deserve it, because I hit first. Everyone saw me hit first. Years of imitating how I try to read, years of grabbing at the edges of my clothes, but because everyone saw my fist go into him first, everything after is on me.

I forgot, at the worst possible moment, that someone like me doesn't get to fight back.

# BASTIÁN

Lore," I say again. Even though I can't understand the name they're saying above the rushing water, I can hear it enough to know it's not mine.

Lore clutches the edges of the desk they're on, pupils wide enough to take up most of their irises.

"It's me, okay?" I say.

Lore stares at me. I think I hear the beginning of a name, my name this time. But the motion of what looks like a wall coming at us stops us both.

I grab Lore's arm and pull them with me before a cabinet crushes us against the desk. We get out of the way just as the cabinet slams into it, wooden panels rattling.

With that noise, Lore flinches, clicking back into right now.

The rising water has turned the ground floor of where the Garcias live into an obstacle course. The mess of half-finished furniture, some upright, some upended, knocks together, pieces bouncing off one another. Knots of water-weed grab at chair legs and the corners of tables. Stray blotches of paint light up like they're under ultraviolet.

I bang into the hard corner of something, a low piece of furniture that probably has a fancy name, but I don't know it. As pain spreads through my shin, I push it away hard enough to shift its path, and the water carries it toward the wall.

Lore pulls me toward the door, getting us out of the way of a cluster of chairs. They bob along on a stand of kelp that shifts colors under the water.

We follow the rush of the current out onto the sidewalk. The foam on the dark water flashes orange as wild poppies.

We run into the middle of the street, and the water thins out enough that it doesn't go past our ankles. Water thyme and star grass float past us. Pieces catch on our shoes.

"Are you okay?" I ask.

Lore looks around. Their wet hair gathers into pieces and falls into their face.

"I made a mistake," they say. "I screwed everything up."

"Hey." Lore still hasn't let go of me, so I don't let go

either. I slide my hands under their elbows, trying to get them to look at me. "This wasn't your fault. None of this is your fault."

But Lore's not hearing me. They watch the pieces of water thyme gather around our feet.

"Do you do hugs?" I ask.

Lore looks up with a laugh, like I caught them off guard. "What?"

"I don't know if you do hugs, so I'm asking." I didn't expect this to be funny, but Lore's still laughing, so I'll take it.

"Sure," Lore says.

I'm not a natural hugger, not like most of my family is. When I was little and people tried to hug me without asking, it was sometimes the thing that pushed me from agitated into overstimulated. Hugs I didn't want made me hide in the cabinets under sinks, in garages, in the back seat of the car our neighbor always forgot to lock, anywhere I thought no one would find me.

But the longer we stay like this, the more we figure out how our bodies fit together, the more I relax into it. My arms cross Lore's back. Lore's palms spread out over my shoulder blades. Lore's forehead rests against my shoulder.

Lore lifts a piece of star grass out of my hair, the strand of thin leaves dotted with tiny yellow flowers. Then I'm laughing with them, and I figure that's when we'll pull apart. We'll take this off-ramp to end the hug.

But Lore doesn't pull back. I don't either. Even though water and lake plants are winding around where we stand, even though the hems of our jeans are deeper blue from the water soaking them, I don't want to. Even though we're both looking over each other's shoulders for any sign of a seiche, I want this.

For one of the few times I can remember, I not only stay still, I want to.

# LORE

When it's over, and the world goes back, things almost look normal. The folding chairs we're working on for the wedding aren't tangled together. The cabinets aren't warped and waterlogged. The desk hasn't splintered into pieces.

But something's off.

Everything's in a slightly different place than before.

I shift them, so slowly that they barely grind against the floor. I try to get them as close to where they were without waking up my parents. In the morning, my parents may blink at each of them, wondering if a credenza sidled up to a bookshelf when no one was looking. But I'll just keep working, like I don't even notice. If they ask about it, I'll laugh. *What, you think the furniture's throwing wild parties while we sleep?*

I hear the faint edges of a voice from upstairs. I swear under my breath, wondering which of my parents I just woke up. In a minute one of them will be on the stairs with a bleary expression and an unfiltered, *What the hell are you doing, Lore? It's three in the morning.*

The sound thickens and sharpens.

The pitch of it crawls along my neck, and it resolves into a high, taunting laugh.

My hands grip the dresser, palms clammy against the wood.

I stay still, my breath rasping in my throat. I shut my eyes tight.

The laugh shimmers along the walls, like the sound is swallowing me. It's still quiet, as though whoever is laughing is holding a hand over their mouth to muffle the sound. But it feels so close I'm wearing it. It's coating my skin.

I stay still. I clench my teeth and fold my tongue against my soft palate.

The laugh fades.

I take a gasping breath in, knowing what I need to do.

I have to tell Bastián.

# BASTIÁN

"What do you want?" I stand at the edge of the world under the lake. I hate how exasperated my voice is. I sound like I'm trying to reason with a temperamental cat who has already decided I am beneath her.

The weather in my brain is drying out. Any rain or mist is evaporating.

"Do you want me to make you new friends?" I ask. "Is that it?"

As though I don't make enough alebrijes, every time I have one of my bad days, every time I make a mistake I can't stop thinking about.

The horses and axolotls glide toward me and then hover. I flinch and back up. But then I realize they're not trying to rush toward the surface.

They're trying to get me to come to them.

"No," I say. "I'm not coming down there."

I step back. I'm not going near these living versions of my worst days.

"I can't," I say. "And you know that."

# LORE

'm worried," Bastián's mother—the one who told me
to call her Ava—says when she answers the front door.

All I get out is "uh . . ." before she keeps going.

"They're in a rabbit hole," she says. "Hiperconcentración.
You get them out of the house and into daylight, I'll give
you whatever you want. Do you smoke? What brand?"

"I don't smoke," I say.

"Good." Her face turns intense and forbidding. "That
was a trick question. You shouldn't smoke. Never start."

I step back and respond with an encore, "Uh . . ."

"They've been in that room for years," she says.
"Years. Planets have been demoted in less time."

Ava Silvano should go up against my mother in the
sport of exaggeration. *Will you turn this down, it's five thousand degrees in here.*

Bastián has not been in that room for years; they were at work earlier today. I know because I thought about stopping into the copy-print place on the way home but couldn't think of a good excuse by the time I got close enough that they might see me. I saw them, a flash of their hair and their shirt, before I ran back around the corner. Like the coward I am.

"Go." Ava points down the hall. "See if you can get them out and into the living world."

I do what I'm told. On principle and from experience, I don't argue with Mexican mothers.

When Bastián sees me in the doorway to their room, how fast they stand up from their desk chair almost makes me laugh, like they're in an old movie, rising for the entrance of someone important. "I thought you were coming over at"—Bastián checks the clock—"oh."

"Yeah," I say. "Sorry, your mom said you were in here. Well, more accurately, she said you were in hyperfocus."

Bastián laughs at that, but seems a little on edge. They look around their room, self-conscious as though there were dirty clothes and snack wrappers everywhere. But nothing's especially out of place. There's a jacket on the dresser. A stack of books on the floor that look like they just came from the library or are about to get returned. Their bed's made in only the most half-assed way, but no one I know except my mom whole-ass makes their bed every day, complete with redoing the corners.

A breeze through the open window rustles a corkboard full of postcards. They're packed in, overlapping like fish scales, and they're all some kind of art. A pink shell by Georgia O'Keeffe. A photo of a miniaturized room, complete with tiny furniture. Edmonia Lewis's sculpture of Cleopatra.

"I like your collection," I say.

"Yeah." Bastián clears their throat. What am I doing that's making them so nervous? "Those are from my brother. We send them back and forth."

"You and your brother are pen pals?" I ask. "That's adorable."

"My brother's fifteen years older than me," Bastián says. "Most of my memories of him growing up are after he moved out."

I track Bastián's eyes twitching around the room. Did last night make things irreparably, universally weird?

As I watch where Bastián's looking, I notice the small details of their room I missed. I count seven alarm clocks and timers, some shaped like cubes, others like a tomato or a cat. All the clocks are ahead of the kitchen clock I just saw, either by a few minutes or almost twenty, but none of them say exactly the same time as any other one. Index cards are taped to light switches and the edges of the dresser and tacked to more squares of corkboard. I can't tell what they say, though. The handwriting on them, each a short phrase, maybe a sentence, is looping and artistic but unintelligible to me. The same dyslexia that gives me messy handwriting makes it harder for me to understand other people's handwriting.

They notice me noticing, and tamped-down horror crosses their face. So I set my focus on one thing they're not looking at nervously, the paints and paper and brushes on their desk. Alebrijes crowd the space in front of them.

"Did you really make all those?" I ask.

Bastián hesitates before saying, "Yeah," under their breath.

"They're incredible," I say. An orange rabbit wears a shell of sea urchin's spines. A raccoon has tiny plastic jewels for eyes. A brush soaked with ultramarine paint rests next to a fox with a jellyfish tail.

Bastián still looks uncomfortable.

"Do you want me to leave?" I ask.

"No," Bastián says, and they say it fast enough that I'm pretty sure they mean it.

The air through the window comes in stronger, lifting the index cards like leaves.

I still can't read most of them, but the breeze tilting up toward the light lets me read some.

*Drink water.*

*Take meds.*

*Slow down.*

*Breathe.*

*Write it down.*

*Do one thing at a time.*

*Breathe again.*

*If you don't write it down, it doesn't exist.*

*Where are your keys?*

*Don't forget your water bottle.*

*No, really, you're on T now. Don't forget your water bottle.*

That's when I get it.

Bastián doesn't think their room is a mess.

Bastián didn't want me to see the index cards. For whatever reason, their room has dozens of these, each reminding them about something. And the reason could be anything. It could be things they've told me show up in a brain like mine. Trouble with working memory. Processing and retrieval problems. Possible detail in support of this theory: There's some kind of filled-out form in the middle of Bastián's floor, which makes me wonder if Bastián does the same trick I do, placing things I need to take with me so they're literally in my way. My choices are either to remember to bring it or trip over it, so I do this with anything important that isn't breakable or a potentially hazardous obstacle.

I want to ask. Of course I want to ask. But it's none of my business. And even if it was, how would I ask? *Hey, random question, but did you grow up thinking there was maybe something weird about your own brain? Or that your brain was doing things the wrong way? That* you *were doing things the wrong way?*

Even in my head, it sounds like a bad infomercial. It comes with a flourish of harp sounds. *There's an Amanda the Learning Specialist for that.*

I look around for something else to comment on.

Next to their bed, a jar of blue-violet water holds a layer of sparkles at the bottom. The sun lights it up like a fish tank.

"That's shiny," I say. "What is it?"

"It's a glitter jar." Bastián grabs it and puts it in my hands. "You have to shake it up."

That seems to relax them a little. They don't even seem to notice that the paint on their hands just left strokes of color on the glitter jar.

So this subject is safe. I make a mental note.

I watch the green and coral sparkles spin through the water.

As I turn the jar over, I notice more color on the bookshelf. The pack of alebrijes isn't just on the desk. The alebrijes have spilled onto the shelves, each either half-painted or all the way finished. They've overrun the windowsill, crowding next to paints and brushes and coils of wire. Alebrijes sit on top of newspaper on Bastián's dresser. A tortoise with owl's wings. A purple cat with a peacock's tail. A coyote with a hummingbird's markings and fins behind the ears.

Their coats all shine like they're just painted, no films of dust on any of them. No wonder the window's open.

I'm so used to the smell of paint and varnish and other nonpolar solvents that I barely notice them, but when the breeze turns, I catch the subtle sharpness of acrylic paint.

I'm now seeing what Ava saw.

In the least alarmed voice I have, I ask, "What are you doing?"

"I missed something." Bastián paces between the desk and the bed, which isn't a lot of space, so it gives the effect of them knocking between the walls of a pinball machine. "I had to have missed something. There's something I was supposed to send down there that I didn't, and now it's pulling everything else up here, and I can't figure out what it is."

So I'm not the only one who sometimes feels like I'm fighting my own brain.

The pinch of last night comes back. Sending those ribbons of paint into the dark made me think I was doing the right thing. But I made the world under the lake volatile and dangerous. It came above the surface and threw my worst memories back at me. It didn't accept them like it did with Bastián.

"I don't think you're the problem," I say.

Bastián picks up another wire frame from the desk. "What do you mean?"

"I think there's something wrong where my family's living," I say.

Bastián's fingers leave paint smudges on the wire skeleton. "What kind of wrong?"

"Like something in those rooms isn't happy," I say. "Like the rooms or the walls themselves aren't happy."

Bastián stares at me.

"Every time the world under the lake comes above the surface," I say, "I hear something."

"What kind of something?" I say.

I anticipate how flimsy this will sound. "A laugh. One that feels like it's right next to me but also like it's coming from far away. Like I'm hearing it through water. I don't think it's one of my neighbors, and I keep hearing it, especially when the world under the lake shows up. So I'm starting to wonder if there's some kind of connection."

Bastián's eyes fall shut.

"You think I sound ridiculous," I say.

"No," Bastián says. "It's not that. It's that Abril's going to be insufferable. Come on."

"Where are we going?" I ask.

Bastián goes toward the door. "To ask someone who might know something."

# BASTIÁN

"Proceed with caution." I lead Lore over the contours of the rocks.

"Where are we?" Lore asks.

"Somewhere we're not exactly supposed to be," I say.

A sliver of water catches the sun.

"I thought you wanted me to stay away from the lake," Lore says.

"Yeah," I say. "Because that plan's working."

We go over the crest of the rocks, the floor of the bight veined with old roots.

The rocks shift, and Lore loses their footing.

"Careful." I hold out my hand. Lore only grabs it for a second before they're steady again, but when I see their fingers on my forearm, I realize how much paint is still on me. Green and orange and blue cross the brown of my skin. One habit I haven't broken is doing a rushed, shoddy job washing off paint. It takes forever under the tap, and my patience thins out faster than the acrylic.

Lore surveys the bight in front of us, the swing sets, climbing bars, the worn-wood playhouse with a ladder and slide.

They look back at the wall of rocks we just climbed over.

"Weird place for a playground," Lore says.

"It's kind of not a playground anymore," I say. "It was, but after the last big storm all those rocks crashed in, so it's not kid safe at the moment."

I only have to wait a few seconds for my friends to come out of the playhouse.

Sloan stands at the open side. He has on one of the graphic T-shirts he wears so much the design is pilling off.

"That's not even one of the options," he's saying to Vivienne.

"I don't care." Vivienne sits on the edge of one slide. "I want her wardrobe."

"You're basing this on costume design?" Sloan asks.

"Hey," Maddie says. "It's one of the great art forms of cinema. Without it, the visual cohesion of a film doesn't work."

Abril sits at the top of the other slide, legs crossed in. "She's right. You hear actors all the time talking about how when they put on the clothes, they become the character."

As the debate continues, I glance between each of them and Lore. "That's Sloan. That's Maddie. You already know Vivienne and Abril."

"Back me up on this," Sloan says, not hearing us.

I missed what Sloan was just saying, but whatever it is, I go with, "I'm not taking sides here."

"That's right," Abril says. "Bastián's too much of a Libra to pick a favorite." She looks at me. "No offense."

I hold my hands up, in a gesture that probably looks like *no offense taken* but that I hope conveys *please leave me out of this*. Avoiding conflict is the best strategy for me. When I get pulled into arguments, even about ranking a movie franchise, I stop planning out what I'll say. When I say things without thinking, I say the wrong things.

"You." Sloan looks at Lore.

"They do have a name," Vivienne says.

"This is Lore," I say.

Sloan ignores me and keeps looking right at Lore. "Favorite of the original trilogy."

I'm about to say *You don't have to answer that*, but Lore answers, fast, "First one."

"And why is that?" Sloan says. With him up on the playhouse, I feel like we're both standing before some kind of judge and reasoning with a child to come down from the rope ladder.

"Most R2-D2 screen time," Lore says. "After the first time my parents showed it to me, I went around beeping like that for months. But they figured they'd brought it upon themselves so they didn't stop me. Especially when they realized I was so annoying I could get people they didn't like to leave."

Everyone laughs except Vivienne, who catches my eye and mouths, *I like them*.

I don't know why it takes this to make it clear to me, but it's now clear to me: Lore is *weird*. A kind of weird possibly in the same universe as the kind of weird I am.

"I deem your reasoning worthy," Sloan says.

Lore gives the most sarcastic bow I've ever seen, eyes wide and eyebrows raised.

The whole time Lore talks with my friends, I'm only partly hearing them.

Mostly, I'm thinking about what Lore saw in my room. The reminder notes I put everywhere. Along with timers and alarms that help me do what I need to do but might forget. They remind me what I need for the next day. They cue me to hydrate. They help me not interrupt myself in the middle of completing tasks, like half finishing the dishes and then starting dinner and then forgetting about both and taking a shower.

They give me shorthand versions of classes and therapy sessions, so I remember to put the brakes on my own brain. *Slow versus fast. Hot versus cold. Next step first.*

Lore's not asking about them. But I bristle at the thought that anyone but Mom and Mamá and Antonio and my closest friends have seen them, the kind of adjustments I have to make to compensate for everything my brain either can't do or resists doing.

I have to shift out of thinking about this. That's not why we're here. Shoving my brain off this train of thought feels like putting all my weight behind moving a piece of furniture. It doesn't budge, and then all of a sudden, it slides, and I'm blurting out, "Abril, can Lore and I talk to you for a minute?"

Everyone looks at me, and I know I just interrupted.

Abril comes down the slide. "You requested an audience?"

I wait for the conversation above to get loud enough that no one will hear us.

I look at Lore.

"Bastián says you know about something about where I live," Lore says.

"What do you mean?" Abril asks. Then it clicks, and she beams at me. "Bastián Silvano, are you admitting I'm right?"

I glance at Lore. "I told you she'd be like this."

Lore ignores me. "Yes, they're admitting you're right. Now what do I do?"

"You did tell them I don't know how to un-haunt things, right?" Abril asks me.

"So it is haunted?" Lore asks. Alarm sharpens their voice. "It's definitely haunted?"

I glare at Abril. "Thanks. Thanks for that."

"What do I do?" Lore says. "It's like the walls don't like that I'm there."

Abril frowns.

Lore looks nervous. Lore doesn't know that this is Abril's thinking frown. Hope isn't lost yet.

"I need to do a little research," Abril says.

"Research?" I ask.

"Asking my grandmother a few questions," Abril says. "I'll let you know what I find out."

"Thank you," Lore says.

"No, thank you." Abril grins at me. "I didn't think I'd win this debate."

"Hey, Lore," Sloan calls down. "We have follow-up questions."

Lore takes a few steps to get a clear line of conversation with Sloan, Maddie, and Vivienne.

Lore plays with their hands as they talk, twisting their fingers together in front of them. I can't stop watching. Their hands. Their face. Their braids brushing their shoulders.

"What are you standing here for?" Abril says, low enough that no one can hear. "Go over there."

"They saw the index cards," I say, fast. Not fast because I didn't mean to say it. Fast because I want it over with.

Abril looks at me with a wince of sympathy. She's one of the few people outside my family who know what this means.

Abril knows that tangible reminders like the index cards are part of the external scaffolding of my life. They help me remember things in the moment I need to do them. They're also never the same between one time Abril comes over and the next.

Sometimes things staying the same are good—when I take my meds, putting my keys in the same place, cleaning the papers out of my bag at the end of the week. But sometimes things staying the same means they stop working. If I left the index cards the same, I'd go right by them without even seeing them. So I rearrange them the same way I rearrange the clocks and alarms. I write the words and phrases in different colors. I cut the cards into different shapes. I switch them around. I make patterns and then take them apart. If they look different, then I notice them. I drink a glass of water, and I pause long enough to calm down. I open the notebook I carry around and look back at what I wrote down.

That doesn't mean I want Lore to know any of this.

"How do I explain that?" I ask.

"You either don't," Abril says, "because you don't have to. You don't owe anyone an explanation. Or you tell them the truth, that you've worked incredibly hard to work with your brain."

I feel myself frowning, not because I don't appreciate what Abril just said—I do—but because sometimes compliments make me uncomfortable. Even ones I want to be true.

"If it makes you feel any better," Abril says, "I put the chances of them reacting badly at about 0.3 percent."

"Just as a rough estimate?" I ask.

"Precisely calculated with science," she says. "I'm even better at math than you, you know that. And anyway"—Abril's whisper goes even lower—"if that 0.3 percent is the case, they're not worth it. They're not worth you."

Abril kicks at the heel of my shoe, and it startles me into stumbling. She knows me well enough to know I'll try to make it look deliberate by walking forward. Which gets me close to Lore. The only not-awkward way I can explain coming toward them is to take the swing next to them.

Abril climbs back up the wooden ladder. When her entrance shifts the center of the conversation back up to the playhouse, Lore reaches for their bag.

"I brought something to show you." Lore opens a book and hands it to me. "See?" They tap the glossy page. The spread shows glow-in-the-dark green cats in an olive-green kitchen. "*Radioactive Cats*."

I trace my fingers over the page, outlining the cats.

"Did you know a group of jellyfish is called a bloom?" I ask.

I realize, only after I've said it, that this was too fast of a conversation change. Just because the connection was clear in my head—cats, colorful cats, colorful animals, jellyfish—doesn't mean it would be clear to anyone else.

"Yeah," Lore says. "I did know that one."

"And it's called a thunder of hippopotamuses," I say.

"Didn't know that one," Lore says.

"And a dazzle of zebras," I say.

"Oh, I like that one," Lore says.

I stop. One more and it'll be clear I looked all these up to impress Lore.

I turn the pages, from the green cats I've been staring at, to a scene of a bright turquoise bedroom swarmed by orange goldfish. A pack of red foxes invades a dining room that's gray right down to the chandelier. Then comes a house as pink as a doll's dress, with a bluish-lavender interior, and dozens of midnight-blue squirrels and a few ink-black crows.

There are people in the frames, but my eyes don't go to them. They look bored, incidental, like they're background noise to what's happening, and everything that's happening is background noise to them.

"I love that one," Lore says, pointing to the page I've just paused on, a flurry of ultramarine-blue leaves whirling through an autumn-brown room.

"I forget things sometimes," I blurt out. "Really basic things."

What is wrong with me today? Two socially inappropriate subject changes in a row. *Nicely done, Bastián. Care to try for a third?*

Lore pauses for a second, and I think they'll say something like, *That came out of nowhere.* But they say, "Everyone does."

"I appreciate you saying that, and I know you're trying to be nice," I say. "But when I say I forget things, I mean, a lot. I forget to eat, and then I'm somehow surprised when I'm really hungry. I forget that I'm holding something, so I'll drop it or spill it or break it. My long-term memory, it's pretty good. Like I remember what color shirt you were wearing when we met. It was orange."

"No, it wasn't," Lore says.

"No, not when we met the other day," I say. "The actual first time we met."

Lore's eyes open a little more. "Wow."

"Yeah," I say. "But that's my long-term memory. My working memory, it's shit. I can't hold much in my head at once."

Lore looks down at our feet and the hems of our jeans. "You're talking about the cards."

I look down too. "Yeah."

Most of the time, I don't like quiet very much. It

scares me. It gives my thoughts too much space to ricochet around. But the quiet Lore lets stand between us, I need that. I don't realize I need it until it's there, open, not filled with compassion or commentary. I said something I needed to say, and now Lore knows, and that's all it needs to be.

Lore twists in the swing, left and right. Their shirt pulls tighter against them. Lore's chest is flatter than it sometimes is, enough that they must be wearing a binder. It's the kind of thing I don't want to notice but do, especially since I wear binders.

"What are your words?" I ask, and then immediately wonder if that was enough time for a subject change.

"What do you mean my words?" Lore asks.

"Like how I'm nonbinary, and I'm also a boy, a guy," I say. "Do you have words that feel right?"

"*Boy* is usually a pretty good bet," Lore says. "On select days, so is *girl*."

"I'm never a girl," I say.

"Yeah, I guessed that," Lore says. "But I don't love guessing, and I don't really love when people guess with me, so thanks for telling me."

The air shifts, and I can smell Lore's soap, the artificial fruit of raspberry or apple shower gel.

"When did you come out?" I ask.

"A few years ago?" Lore says. "Before I told my parents, I was going to school looking like a girl every day, and if I wasn't feeling girly that day, I'd change when I got to school and then change back before I went home."

"Wow," I say. "That is closet-committed."

"You have no idea." Lore kicks at the rocks. "Once I was in full boy mode, hair under the hat, binder and everything, and my mom got home early."

"Oh no," I say.

"Oh yes," Lore says. "I didn't know it was possible to let down my hair that fast, put a bra on under my shirt but over my binder . . ."

"No," I interrupt even though I don't mean to.

"Yes," Lore says. "Easiest way to put my chiches back on after I'd made them disappear." Lore gives a magician's hand flourish. "Then I put on lipstick. All in about a minute. I think I broke the sound barrier."

"You're like the nonbinary Clark Kent." I trace the edges of the book's pages. "Right into the gender phone booth."

"It was a lot like that," Lore says. "Sometimes I kind of wish I could give the people around me a daily report on my gender. Just so they'd know what to expect. So no one would give me that confused look whether I was wearing a binder or makeup or whatever."

When I don't say anything, Lore looks up. "I'm not making any sense, am I?"

"No," I say. "You're making a lot of sense. The world could use daily gender forecasts."

The minute I hear myself say it, I know how stupid it sounds.

But Lore's face lights up. "Yes," they say. "Sunny, forty-two percent expected femininity."

"Tonight," I say, "cloudy with likely masculinity."

"Exactly," Lore says.

Our shoes accidentally touch, my right, Lore's left. I pull back.

When my friends are laughing loudly enough that I'm sure they won't hear, I say what's been stuck in my throat this whole time.

"I'm sorry about everything," I say. "I really thought I could fix it."

Lore looks at me. "You think this is your fault?"

"Well, yeah," I say. "Who else's?"

Lore makes a circle with the toe of their shoe, moving the small rocks out in buckling waves.

"Bastián, I have to tell you something," they say.

"Something other than we have to find a way to calm down the building you're living in?" I ask.

"Yeah," Lore says.

I wait. I don't talk. I want to jump in and ask, *What? What are you talking about?* But sometimes, if the weather in my brain is right, I can give people enough quiet for them to choose the moment they talk. I learned how from watching my brother. Antonio lets silences stand. He lets conversations breathe.

"What happened," Lore says, "with all the furniture and the flooding, that was my fault."

"What do you mean?" I ask. "What are you talking about?"

So much for letting silences stand.

Lore breathes out. "I tried to do what you do, sending things into the world under the lake."

"What?" I turn the swing I'm on toward Lore. "How?"

The book starts sliding off my lap. I forgot I had it. I scramble to keep it from falling, grabbing it by the edge.

"I did what you said you do," Lore says.

"With what?" I ask.

"Paint," Lore says. "I have these paint samples in my room, and when I tried it, I felt it. What you were talking about with letting everything just end up in something small enough that you can hold it. I felt that."

The color in my room.

It was a shadow of the paint Lore gave to the world under the lake.

"But how did you . . ." I don't have the end of the sentence, so it's a relief when Lore interrupts.

"I saw it." Lore pulls closer, pinning themself and their swing still with the toes of their shoes against the ground. "I went to the inlet, and it happened, just like when you showed it to me."

I let my temple fall against one of the swing chains.

"I didn't go down there," Lore says. "I wouldn't do that."

That makes my panic a little smaller. That means there's only so much Lore could have found out.

But the world under the lake still opened for Lore, which means I'm right. Lore's connected to it.

"I'm sorry," Lore says. "I thought it would help, and it didn't."

"It's okay," I say. "It's not your fault."

"You're not mad?"

"No," I say. "Why would I be?"

"Because the world under the lake is yours?"

"It's not mine," I say. "It doesn't belong to me. I'm just the only one I know who's been there. Besides you." I lift my head as another question comes to me. "But what were you trying to send down there?"

Lore opens their mouth, then hesitates.

I know that pause. I've given that pause. That's the *I don't want to talk about it* pause.

"Forget it," I say. "It's none of my business."

I hand Lore back the book.

"You can borrow it if you want," Lore says.

"It's okay." I've gotten better at not losing things. Most of the time I know where my keys, ID, library books are. But the thought of even possibly losing this book, with the pictures Lore stared at growing up, makes me leave it in their hands.

"What if it doesn't work?" Lore asks.

"What?" I ask.

"Sending things down there to get away from them." Lore puts the book in their bag. "What if it doesn't work?"

I feel the shift of weather in my brain, the air drying out. "Can we not talk about this? You tried it. It didn't work. I'm not mad. What have we not covered?"

"But what if it didn't work because it just doesn't work?" Lore asks.

"Lore," I say, slowly, so I can actually think about what I'm saying. "It's the only way it's ever worked for me."

"The only way what's ever worked?" they ask.

"Everything," I say.

Maddie leans over the edge of the slide, tilting her head at Lore. "You know you don't have to listen, right?"

"To what?" Lore asks.

"Bastián's art lectures," Sloan says.

"Other way around." Lore pulls out the book. "This is mine."

Maddie nods. "Carry on."

Lore waits a few seconds for the talking and laughing above us to start back up.

"What if you didn't?" Lore whispers. "What if you don't need to be hiding from whatever you're hiding from?"

"I'm not hiding from anything," I say. "It's how I let things go. That's what people do, right? They let things go. Only it's harder for me to do that, so this is one of the only ways I know how to."

My restlessness, my impulsive moments, the times when I'm overstimulated or overloaded or afraid, putting all those into the alebrijes gives me literal distance from all those things. I don't hate them any more than I hate the alebrijes who carry them in their wings.

They're just not part of me anymore. They can't be.

"I'm not asking what you send down there," Lore says. "But just so you know, I like everything about you."

My hands grip the swing chains, the grain of the rust against my palms.

The version of me that I've worked for years to be—calmer, more careful, a Bastián who thinks about what they'll say before they say it—would take a minute. That Bastián would stay quiet for a few seconds, recognize the compliment, and then respond with *thank you*.

But the version of me I gave over to the world under the lake in pieces, the one that's fast and impulsive and reactive, that Bastián gets to my mouth first.

"You only like everything about me because I don't keep the parts no one would like."

I land on the words hard. It's loud enough that, right after, I know I snapped them at Lore. Just short of yelling.

Lore pulls back, the swing drifting with their shift in weight.

My friends look over the side of the playhouse. They heard me raise my voice, but they look curious, not concerned.

"Disagreement about expressionist painters?" Sloan asks.

Lore produces a laugh that may or may not sound as forced to everyone else as it does to me.

"I've got to get home." Lore stands up from the swing and pulls their bag onto their shoulder. "May the force be with you."

"And also with you," Maddie and Vivienne say in unison.

I watch Lore leave. I watch their swing slow to a stop.

Then I climb up the ladder to meet my friends. I laugh when they laugh. I pretend that I didn't just scare Lore off. I pretend the Bastián I used to be didn't just reach above the surface, and find me, and screw everything up.

I stay up there, sitting on the edge as everyone else goes home. First Maddie and Sloan. Then Vivienne. Then Abril.

"You sure you're okay here on your own?" Abril says.

"I like looking at the water." I tilt my head toward the lake. It's taking on the orange of the sky.

"You just seem a little"—Abril pauses—"brooding."

"I'm fine." My slight laugh seems to satisfy her.

"Okay." But she pauses right before the edge and glances back.

"Go down the damn slide," I say.

Abril gives a quirked smile and whirs down to the ground.

I stay as the sun falls and the sky gets dark. I lean back and lie on the wood platform. I breathe in the smell of stones and dirt, of rotting plants and new growth. I stay long enough that the chill makes me zip my jacket closed. I turn the band of my watch around my wrist, one way, then the other, as I watch the sky.

Whoever said the only things you regret in life are the things you never do probably didn't have ADHD.

When it comes to things I regret, the column of things I've done usually runs longer than the things I haven't. And right now, I regret how I couldn't put the brakes on my own brain and just shut up.

But how do you explain that to someone else? How do you tell someone that you had to work to learn not to follow every impulse your brain has? How do you tell someone that you couldn't just learn it like everyone else does, until it becomes your own common sense? That you came into the world with so much quicksand you needed professional help to learn to steer around it?

My brain won't stop tumbling over what I said to Lore, like water turning a broken piece of a bottle into sea glass. My brain tries to smooth down the edges.

But it keeps stopping in the same place.

When I say things without thinking, I say the wrong things.

Even when the wrong thing is the truth.

*You only like everything about me because I don't keep the parts no one would like.*

It's something I never wanted to say out loud.

But if everything I let go into the world under the lake washes back up, Lore will find out anyway.

# LORE

It happens while I'm walking home. A thread at the center of me lights up and blazes even brighter than how annoyed I am with Bastián.

What the hell was I thinking telling them to do anything when I can't even tell them how my own brain works?

I will never tell Bastián what happened at my last school. I will never tell anyone here. No one here can know any of that if I really want a chance here.

But maybe that doesn't have to apply to everything. Maybe I don't have to tangle all that up with the truth of my brain. Just because Bastián can never know what happened doesn't mean they can never know me.

When I get to the second rung from the top, Bastián hears me, and turns. The moon is still low, and a little gold, trailing a yellow ribbon across the lake. But it gives off enough light to show me Bastián's expression, open, unguarded, but a little shocked to see me.

"If you were trying to scare me off"—I climb onto the wooden platform—"you're gonna have to be a lot more creative than that."

Bastián shifts over. I sit on the edge alongside them. I breathe in the raw, silvery smell of the lake.

"Should I take you not speaking as a bad sign?" I ask.

"Sometimes I shouldn't talk," Bastián says.

"I like when you talk," I say.

"I don't want to talk right now," Bastián says.

"Does that mean you want me to leave?" I ask.

"No." Bastián laughs. "I don't want to talk right now because sometimes I'm an asshole when I talk, in case you haven't noticed."

"No, you're not," I say. "If you were, I wouldn't tell you what I'm about to tell you."

Bastián doesn't look at me. But the way they brace their hands behind them, palms on the wooden planks, lets me know they're listening.

We watch the moon get higher and paler, the ribbon on the water turning to milk. And I try to tell Bastián how my brain works, hoping I'll figure it out as I go.

# LORE

I can't really tell anyone what it's like to be dyslexic. The same as how I can't really tell anyone what it's like to be nonbinary, or Mexican American. I can only tell them what it's like for *me* to be dyslexic.

So this is how I try to explain it to Bastián:

We all have warehouses where our brains store words. People who read without dyslexia—and what puto decided a reading learning disability should have *that* spelling?—they have one really big warehouse, and everything about words gets stored in there. How words are spelled. How they sound. How to read them in your head and out loud.

But for me, it's like I have two totally separate warehouses. One for how words sound, how I hear them and say them. Then another one for how words look on the page, how they're spelled, how I read them. And for every word I know, those two warehouses each have a different item number for it. Take the word *platinum*. I hear that word, and the first warehouse, the hearing/speaking warehouse, goes and gets that word and all the information it knows about it. I know how to say that word out loud. I know how it sounds. I know what it means. When I hear it, it calls up the cold sheen of an expensive ring, or Marilyn Monroe's hair.

But when I come across the word *platinum* on the page, we're not in that first warehouse anymore, the hearing/speaking warehouse that has all that information about blondes and metal. We're in the second warehouse, the reading/writing/spelling warehouse, and all the information I have about that word on the page has to come from that second warehouse, because my brain has attached those two different item numbers to that word, one for how it sounds, and the other for the letters on a page. And because of my dyslexia, it doesn't realize those two item numbers are for the same word. It can't match the letters I'm seeing to a word I've heard a hundred times.

The words I know, I know through memorization. So I match the two item numbers by memory. They're still two different items, but a lot of times I'll remember that they both go to the same word. That's how I learned to read, by memorizing how words looked, by linking them up in my brain even though those two warehouses will never agree on the same inventory system.

If I don't know for sure, I start guessing. I take part of the word and try to match it. Sometimes I guess right, and the reading/writing warehouse finds the right item, *platinum*. But sometimes it pulls the part of the word it recognizes, and I end up thinking or saying *plated* or *platypus*, or other words that may or may not be in the right galaxy as the word on the page. I think our assigned book is *Lord of the Files* instead of *Lord of the Flies*. Or I read out loud in the middle of science class that an octopus has eight testicles, and it takes me a second too long to realize why everyone is laughing. I realize that *platypus blond* is not a thing. A great band name, maybe, but not a thing.

In grade school, some teachers didn't like it when I read by straight memorization. They said "sight reading" like it was dipping a classmate's ponytail into finger paint—the act of a troublemaker. It's okay to do that with certain words, apparently. They call them "sight words." *Little. Yellow. Blue. Mira. Juego. Conmigo.*

But if you try to memorize other words, words you're supposed to *sound out*, then it's called cheating. You're not reading right. And I didn't know how to explain that I couldn't *sound it out* any more than I could have gotten up in front of the class and done thirty-two pirouettes in a row, or broken my desk apart with my bare hands.

A teacher telling me to *just sound it out*—that word *just*, like I was refusing to do something simple—didn't make it any more possible. My brain simply wasn't built for it.

My dyslexia has made me good at memorizing words, at turning every word into a sight word, but abysmal at guessing how a word might sound if I don't know it. An adult could tell me to *just sound it out* all they want, but I'm still going to be dyslexic, and those two warehouses are never going to talk enough to match up their item numbers, to share what they each know about a word. My dyslexia is the scratchy phone lines, glitchy inventory systems, and lost log sheets that make that impossible.

When I stop talking, Bastián doesn't say anything. They don't look at me. But as I've been talking, the tension has been leaving their back and shoulders. Their limbs seem looser now. They're not holding themself quite so rigidly. Their body now knows how to relax while this close to me, enough that when our arms brush, Bastián doesn't pull back.

Tonight, when the world under the lake comes above the surface, it's as quiet as a distant planet. It's bright and dark at the same time, the sky deep violet, the edges of the swings lit up like they're outlined in phosphorescent green. Trails of bubbles float over the lake, each of them as big as pomegranates. They hold ribbons of color that shift between looking like paint and looking like pieces of seaweed.

Instead of a field of silver water, the lake is a seagrass bed that stretches all the way to where we are. The glowing green of the blades drifts in the air, like we're underwater, on the floor of the lake.

When we climb down to the ground, we don't leave right away. We don't go looking for the seiche just yet. We lie in the seagrass meadow. Our fingers find each other in the soft growth, the moon overhead wavering like we're watching it refracted through water.

# BASTIÁN

ost of the time, everything around me is either too quiet or too loud. When there's silence, I'm restless and twitchy. My brain roots around in the stillness, looking for something to pay attention to or wondering what I might be missing. If it's too loud, everything rushes in at once, and I can't filter what's important from what's not.

Some people think ADHD means I can't pay attention, but so often I'm trying to find the point between paying too little attention and paying so much that I get overwhelmed. Finding that point can be as hard as finding a specific star in a whole galaxy. It's trying to pick out the right thread of lightning in an electrical storm. It's cosmic particles colliding. Our brains hold as many cells as the Milky Way contains stars, and sometimes ADHD is like feeling all of them at once, all those cells, all those stars, a whole galaxy of fire and chaos and light.

But right now, every time Lore pauses, every time Lore takes a few seconds or a minute between things they're explaining, my brain doesn't flinch with wanting to fill that quiet. The soft sound of distant lake grass fills it for me. I don't have to remind myself to listen. I'm not going to talk, so I don't have to worry about what I'll say.

It's not like any place—even the world under the lake—or any person—even someone who gets it the way Lore does—will suddenly make my brain different. The sea of underwater grass in front of us, or how the green turns silver as it catches the light, will not make me not have ADHD. Being close to Lore or anyone else cannot and will not change the anatomy or chemistry of my brain.

But for once, I don't have to explain to someone else how my brain works.

For once, someone is explaining theirs to me.

Lore and I look out into what the world under the lake has made of tonight. There's no sound except the drifting of the swings and the whisper of underwater grass and the soft sound of a current around us, like the inside of a shell.

A pair of silver wings flutters down and lands on my sleeve. Another wafts onto Lore's hair. A few more stream over the grass. Lore laughs as an arc of them hover near their shoulder. They surround us the way they did at the edge of the inlet the first time I met Lore.

My brain wants to pick apart what this means. Are we onto something talking to Abril? Are we doing something right, and if so, what is it?

But for just this minute, I set all of that down. I watch the threads of light buckling across our bodies.

We stay still, and they bring us back.

# LORE

**W**hen you have a gender presentation range as wide as I do, you get used to confused looks. I've been walking around here mostly in my work jeans—faded by the wash, flecked with paint—with my hair under hats. But right now I'm wearing one of my more femme-y tops—flowy, embroidered. Red-tinted lip gloss. About as girly as I ever get.

This means every block or so I get a look like someone almost recognizes me. *Is that . . . That looks like Lore . . . That looks like the Garcias' kid . . .* Sometimes they place me by the time I pass them, and they're confident enough to say my name. Sometimes they're not sure, and give the polite, generic smile that works whether they know me or not. It happens three times on the walk to the copy-and-print shop.

I'm considering different rolls of shipping tape—I should have asked my parents to be more specific—when I realize Bastián is a rack of office supplies away from me.

Heat blooms alongside my collarbone, following the embroidery on my shirt. I was almost positive Bastián wasn't on today. Sloan said as much when I ran into him.

I was not planning on Bastián seeing girly Lore.

A name tag glints gold on Bastián's shirt. It doesn't look like their name—I can't read it from this distance but I can tell by the length of the word. But then they get close enough for me to see it's their full first name, Sebastián.

"Are you finding every"—Bastián starts, then I look up, it clicks for them, and Bastián changes course midsentence—"sorry, didn't recognize you."

How level their expression is makes something in me fall and lift at the same time. They're not staring like they think I'm hotter this way than when I dress in my boy clothes, which I appreciate. But maybe they're not staring that way because they don't think of me that way period.

"I thought you weren't working today," I say.

"I'm filling in," Bastián says. "It was last minute." Bastián writes something on a clipboard. "Hey, can you stay around for a second?"

I wave a hand at the rolls of tape. "I'm in the middle of a lengthy deliberation."

"Do you want help?" Bastián says. "Because I can bore you with details about acrylic and hot melt."

"I think I'm up to the challenge," I say. "But thanks."

Bastián disappears, but the sense of them being next to me stays, like the wake after a boat. The slight surprise coming off them is a kind I'm not used to. It was neutral, observant, instead of the thrilled shock of guys seeing me wear makeup for the first time, asking why don't I look this way every day. Once they placed me, Bastián looked at me like I'm just me, like it's not going to be some kind of disappointment if tomorrow I'm wearing my favorite T-shirt and old jeans again.

When Bastián comes back, they hand me a glass jar filled with indigo water.

"It seemed like you liked the ones in my room," Bastián says.

With the motion of being passed from Bastián's hands to mine, green and gold and sherbet-orange glitter swirl through.

"Where do you get these things?" I ask.

"I make them," Bastián says.

I look from the shimmering water to Bastián. "Really?"

"Yeah," Bastián says, like it's nothing. "Why?"

I tilt it back and forth, and it's all my favorite colors at once. The glitter flickers through, and the water shifts purple when I turn it one way, blue when I turn it another.

I think of Bastián dyeing the water, choosing each kind of glitter, sealing the jar.

"So I was thinking about what we were talking about," Bastián says.

"What?" I ask.

"Daily gender forecasts," Bastián says. "What if we do it?"

I turn the glitter jar over. "What do you mean?"

"I mean, whenever we want," Bastián says, "we can just say what our daily forecast is, and then at least someone will know."

"What if I don't know what percentage masculinity's in the forecast?" I ask.

"Then pick anything," Bastián says. "Whatever feels like it says your gender right now. Like, yesterday, I could say my gender was"—Bastián thinks for a minute—"probably a perfectly folded T-shirt."

"Of course it was." I bet all Bastián's T-shirts are perfectly folded. It's one of the things I noticed about their room, the mix of order and chaos. Art supplies cluttered their desk, and flocks of index cards covered their corkboard at all angles, but there weren't clothes left on the floor or scattered around except a stray jacket. Everything I learn about this boy—this boy who maybe folds and puts away their laundry right after washing it but who also doesn't realize when there's paint on their hands—makes me want to learn more about them. And it makes me wonder, even more, if there are similarities between their brain and mine.

"Or maybe my abuelo's dictionary," Bastián says. "Yeah. That's what I'm going with."

As I spin the glitter jar in my hands, I picture what their grandfather's dictionary might look like, the weathered cover, the onionskin. Did Bastián's grandfather make alebrijes like their great-grandfather? Is there paint on the binding and the edges of the pages?

"Your turn." Bastián looks at me. "Gender forecast."

"For right now?" I ask.

"Yeah."

"Right now?" I shake the glitter jar. "I think it might be this."

"Okay." Bastián's smile is shy, and they don't quite look at me, like I've given them some kind of compliment they want but don't know what to do with. "What about yesterday?"

"I guess"—I think about it, how I felt, how to put it in terms other than masculine and feminine, *boy* or *girl*, neither or both or somewhere in the space between—"really strong coffee. Or maybe that popping sound soda makes."

"A gender fizz." Bastián nods. "Sounds like the next big drink."

For a minute, I'm quiet.

When it comes to being trans, so many things can

take the air out of me. The misgendering. The questions about why I can't just be a girl all the time if I can be a girl any of the time. The questions about what got me so confused that I became someone who lives in the space between genders, as though it was that space between that confused me, and not the world's insistence that I live elsewhere.

But this, what Bastián's saying, that look, that puts some of the air back into me.

"None of this would make sense to anyone else," I say.

"So what?" Bastián says. "It doesn't have to make sense to anyone else."

Bastián puts the cap on a permanent marker someone left open near the paper cutter. "The tourists never recap the pens. My sociology observation of the day."

"You get a lot of tourists in here?" I ask.

"A print-and-ship place?" Bastián says. "Oh yeah. Especially this time of year. People staying down the shore with their families come here to do their work stuff."

I turn the glitter jar in my hands again. The sun through the store windows winks off the glitter and throws points of light onto both of us.

"So what about you?" I ask. "What's your current gender forecast?"

"Right now?" Bastián breathes out so slowly the sound gets folded into the rustling of paper. "I think it's a vial of testosterone I don't know what to do with."

"Literally or figuratively?" I ask.

"Literally," Bastián says. "I have it at home, and I just keep staring at it."

"It's a big decision," I say.

"It's not that." Bastián neatens a stack of envelopes near a photo printer. "I made the decision. I already had my first shot."

"Oh," I say. "Then, felicidades?"

"Thanks?" Bastián says, laughing as they imitate the question sound of how I said it.

"Sorry," I say. "I didn't mean it that way. I mean, it sounds like you know this is right for you, so I'm confused. Why the staring at the vial?"

Bastián breathes out again, harder this time. It's officially a sigh. "A nurse gave me my first injection, so that was good. But the clinic is an hour away, so I've got to learn to do them at home. And I'm not great with directions, giving them or following them."

"And yet you work here." I look around at the copiers, printers, scanners. "Each one of these must have an instruction manual a thousand pages long."

"It's adorable that you think I read them," Bastián says.

"You don't?" I ask.

"Not even a little." Bastián pulls out an original someone left in a copier and then cleans the glass plate. "I work on instinct."

"I'm even more impressed now," I say.

"Yeah, except it works until it doesn't," Bastián says. "The directions for my shot, I know I'll get used to them eventually." Bastián sweeps tinsel-sized filaments of paper off the paper cutter. "But they seem so complicated that the complication takes over my brain and I just freeze up."

"They didn't explain it to you during your appointment?" I ask.

"Oh, they did," Bastián says through a worn-out laugh. "I just didn't get it. And I didn't ask the nurse to explain it again, and I should have. She would have gone over it again. I just didn't ask. I never seem to realize how much I should have asked until it's too late."

I can feel Bastián's wince so clearly it presses into my chest plate. I know that feeling of not asking because you don't want to admit that you didn't understand something, that after several more repetitions you still might not understand it, the worry that the other person's patience will thin and fray before you can.

"What about your parents?" I ask.

Bastián hesitates. "They've been really great about everything, but if they're part of this—you know, more than they already have been by just being my parents—then they're gonna ask all the questions. 'Do you feel different now,' 'how do you feel,' 'do you feel okay,' 'are you sure this is safe.' And I don't think they want that any more than I do. I think they're more nervous about it than I am."

"That sounds like a lot," I say.

"It's been less than a week and they look at me like they're listening for my voice to crack, and it's making me really tense." Bastián drops a few of the stray paper clips they're collecting.

I pick them up, our fingers brushing as I slip them into Bastián's hand. We both look up at the same time. I look away, fast, before I know if Bastián does the same thing.

"I just don't want it to be a big deal." Bastián gathers up a few more errant paper clips, some rubber bands. "And I don't want this to be the thousandth thing they have to help me with."

"Then let me," I say.

The words are out of my mouth on impulse, and seeing the shocked look on Bastián's face, I wish I could pull them back.

"Are you serious?" Bastián asks, but they sound more hopeful than shocked.

"If you want," I say. "I'm pretty good with directions."

Not exactly a lie. I'm great with directions as long as I'm hearing them and not reading them. Pictures help. I'm really hoping there are pictures.

"I don't mean the shot," I say. "I mean the figuring-it-out part. I can help you with the shot if you want, but you'd have to be okay with me seeing"—I check to make sure no one's close enough to listen, or waiting for Bastián to help with a copier—"whatever part of you we're working with."

Bastián looks at me a little oddly. "My leg?"

"You can do it in your leg?" I ask.

"That's where the nurse gave me my first one, yeah."

This all just got simultaneously more and less awkward.

"Why do you look so relieved?" Bastián says.

"No reason," I say.

"Wait." Bastián starts laughing. "Were you willing to put a syringe in my ass?"

"Shut up," I say. "That's where I thought they went. That's where they told me back when I was thinking about it. No, really, shut up."

"I didn't say anything," Bastián says, but they're clearly making an effort not to laugh.

"Okay, but your face right now," I say.

"My face?" Bastián says. "You should see yours. It's priceless." Bastián looks at me, right at me, and we're close enough that I can see a slight red tint to their eyes that only shows in direct sunlight, a warmth in the brown.

Why do I feel this off-kilter right now, when we've been in a world that doesn't exist to anyone else? Why do I have trouble looking at this boy now when our hands have found each other in seagrass?

Bastián watches the refracted light from the glitter. "You're sure you don't mind?"

"Yeah," I say. "Just tell me when."

My hands turn the jar, and it looks like it holds stardust or a sunset. The glitter sends fireflies of green and yellow light over our faces and chests.

"Sebastián," says a woman holding her hand over the microphone half of a desk phone. "Machine three's out of legal-size."

Bastián cuffs up their sleeves and says in a voice filled with theatrical gravitas, "This is my chance to shine."

I give an equally serious nod. "Godspeed."

# LORE

Abril's deliberations over a new conditioner make my tape selection look rushed.

"I asked my grandmother," she says, "and here's what I found out."

She tells me the building has a long history of lakelore. One fall, orange sunburst lichen grew on the side of the building, perfectly predicting the storms that season. Another year, it was angry about beautiful stones being taken from the shore, and the curb in front tripped every tourist who had coyamito agate in their pockets. Ten years after that, people insisted that when the weather and the moon and the seiches were right, pools opened up in the sidewalk, like rings cut in ice, revealing opaleye and mooneye fish swirling underneath.

"My abuela doesn't really believe that last one," Abril

says. "The point is, it's always been a house with a lot of feelings."

So this was long enough ago that it was one enormous house, before they divided the building into units.

"So what do I do?" I ask.

Abril smells a bottle with the attention of a perfumer. "My grandmother says to fluff the pillows."

I don't even try not to stare. "What?"

"Not literally." Abril puts the bottle back. "Well, yes, literally. But not just the pillows. She says open the curtains. Smooth down the corners of the wallpaper. Show you care. She says sometimes ghosts and unsettled spaces just need to be shown a little consideration."

"And that works?" I ask.

"My abuela knows this stuff," Abril says. "Once her sister moved into the house and kept losing things. They would just disappear from right where she left them. Then my grandmother found out that the original owner had painted the house coral because it was her favorite color and she wanted to live inside her favorite color. But then when she died, the next owners had painted it a different color, and the place got really angry. When my grandmother convinced her sister to paint it back, everything was fine."

"I'll try it," I say, not adding *I'll try anything.*

Abril picks up a bottle that's raspberry-scented, the conditioner tinted pink. "I meant to ask you. Did you tell me how you and Bastián met?"

"It was a long time ago," I say.

Abril keeps looking at me. Her expressions says *I'll wait.*

"I was here on a field trip," I say, "and I was kind of hiding from someone. That's when I met Bastián. At the lake."

A light comes on in Abril's eyes. "That was you?"

"What?" I ask.

Bastián told her about me? Us meeting was significant enough for them to tell a friend, and for that friend to remember?

Abril looks startled, like she just realized her mistake.

In an attempt to dispel the awkwardness of this moment, I grab a bottle of the conditioner my mom and I have both used for three years. "Try this."

Abril smells it. "I like it." I have no idea if she means it or is just trying to help with the awkwardness, but either way, I'll take it.

I go home. And every time I take breaks from sanding and painting, I circle the rooms, dusting windowsills and smoothing the curling edges of old wallpaper. I scrub marks off door frames and dust the top of the fridge. I take the glass cover off each ceiling light and wash it in the bathroom sink. I show all the consideration I can, hoping it might settle these rooms and that chilling laugh.

# BASTIÁN

**W**hen Lore comes over, I'm in the kitchen, sitting on top of the fridge.

Lore looks up at me. "Should I ask?"

"You're the one who just talked to Abril," I say. "Should *I* ask?"

"We're trying something," Lore says.

I hand Lore the directions I'm studying and climb down. "Did you know a group of salamanders is called a maelstrom?"

Lore stands back while I jump down from the counter.

"I can't read these," Lore says.

"Oh," I say. "Right. Sorry."

"I mean, I can read them." Lore washes their hands at the sink, the soap fluffing on their hands. "But I won't get much of them unless you want to stand around while I read them about ten more times. Maybe not actually ten, but if you're standing there watching me, that's gonna make me nervous and reading already makes me nervous, so now that I think of it, yes, maybe ten. So can you read them out loud?"

I read them all the way through, out loud.

Lore has their eyes closed off and on, occasionally handling the syringe, the needles, the prep pads I've set out.

"One more time, okay?" Lore asks when I get to the end.

I read them through again, same speed.

"I think I've got it," Lore says when I finish.

"What do you mean, you've got it?" I ask.

"I have a weirdly good memory," Lore says. "Once I understand something, I remember it. But if this is practice, what are we injecting into?"

I hold up a bag of damaged oranges that fell off a neighbor's tree, and that she was more than happy to have me gather off her lawn. "Sorry it's not my ass. I really hate to disappoint you."

"I'm sure your ass is magnificent." Lore opens an alcohol prep pad. "But I'll be okay." Lore grabs an orange and swipes the pad over it.

"You're sanitizing the fruit?" I ask.

"Hey." Lore holds it up, a patch of the rind shining from the alcohol. "For our purposes, this is you. You do this exactly like you're supposed to do on you. Be the orange."

"I admire your dedication," I say.

"Say it." Lore holds the fruit closer to my face. "I am the orange."

"I am the orange," I repeat. I run an alcohol pad over another orange.

"Good," Lore says. "Then you'll be ready when the orange is you."

We unwrap the practice syringes and put on the blunt fill needles for drawing.

"Are you really not gonna tell me why you were on top of the fridge?" Lore asks.

"I just like climbing things," I say. "Counters, trees, tops of fridges. Sitting still's not really my thing. Going up there"—I glance toward the top of the fridge—"used to help me see things differently when I was a kid. It calmed me down."

"You did that as a kid?" Lore asks.

"Oh yeah." I pat the counter. "This kitchen's got a good setup for it."

Lore takes me through the next steps slowly enough—with enough patience for each time I ask *Wait, can you say that part again?* and *Can you back up a little?*—that they start to flow together.

"If you were actually doing this with the vial"—Lore

checks one of the pictures—"this would be when you turned it upside down to draw down the dose."

Lore talks me through drawing into the syringes, what's the same, what'll be different when I'm drawing with the vial. I watch Lore's hands, their fingers confident, unhesitating. I copy what they do.

"But what made you think of it in the first place?" Lore asks. "Climbing the fridge."

I watch the saline fill the barrel.

We switch out the needles, the thicker-drawing ones for the thinner kind I'll inject with. The needle I will eventually pull into my leg is about an inch and a half long. But that thought is far less intimidating than saying the words I say next.

"I have ADHD."

"Oh." Lore sounds not repelled, not shocked, more like they're putting something together.

"Yeah," I say.

This was a terrible idea. The more complicated things are, the less I want to explain them. It's not just that my brain has trouble organizing things, though that's certainly part of it. It's that I get frustrated with how long it takes it explain them, how much you have to stop and backtrack and clarify. A particular cord of muscle in my back tenses up thinking of telling my parents I wanted to start testosterone. Not because they tried to talk me out of it—they didn't; they just wanted to understand. And it's not that I didn't want them to understand—I did.

But the process of explaining things wears out my brain. I want to take everything I'm thinking and just throw it all out there at once, like upending the contents of a box. But conversations don't work that way. And it's not lost on me how ironic it is that I don't want to explain things even as I need things repeatedly explained to me. That's where resisting my first impulse comes in. My first impulse is *screw it, not worth it.* But I set that aside, and instead, I do the math.

Right now, this is the math: I want Lore to understand. And if I want that, I have to explain. I want Lore to understand more than I want to get out of explaining this.

"It was a little hard to catch because before I came out," I say, "I was kind of socialized like a girl, and because of how girls are socialized, in class I mostly seemed out there and daydreamy. That just doesn't flag people for ADHD as fast."

Lore cringes. "The gender binary strikes again."

"Yeah," I say, sighing. "The restlessness, the fidgeting, the distraction, the impulse control stuff, the stuff you'd expect with ADHD, it's all here. I've just learned to keep it on the inside."

Lore holds the needle up to the light. "That sounds hard."

I want to tell them that sometimes it's okay, and

sometimes it's exhausting. Sometimes it means trying to change the weather in my own brain and finding it as impossible as moving the clouds in a storm. The weather in my brain may or may not match up with what's going on, but an atmosphere of something being wrong can permeate everything even if I can't figure out what it is.

Sometimes it means not saying anything when someone misgenders me because I don't want to be flagged as a problem any more than I already am. So when it happens, I absorb it, take the impact, give the right reassuring looks to my friends so they'll know to stand down, I don't want them starting a fight for me.

Sometimes the way my brain can't filter out what's important from what's not—what looks in the hall are directed toward me and which have nothing to do with me, which noises I need to alert to and which I should ignore—feels so big I can't hold it steady. It's a buoy I'm constantly trying to push underwater. It takes all my effort, all my weight, and even then I'm usually only doing a half-assed job. But a half-assed job is also better than I'd be doing without therapy and class and the medication that gives my brain just enough of a filter to remember what I'm supposed to be doing.

Sometimes it's meant collapsing in on myself to hide the noise in my own brain. Sometimes it's left me wound so tight I feel like I'm grinding down my own gears.

Sometimes it's meant burning my own heart to the

ground to make sure the way my brain disrupts me doesn't disrupt anyone else.

What I say instead: "You get used to it."

"Getting used to something doesn't make it easy," Lore says.

Lore saying that feels like a latch clicking open, something unlocking. Like there's space for me to tell the truth.

"When I first got diagnosed," I say, "my parents didn't want to tell me."

"Why?" Lore asks.

"Because they thought knowing would make me feel different in a bad way," I say. "Like me knowing would make it worse."

"What, like those old cartoons?" Lore asks. "When they accidentally run off the cliff but don't fall until they look down?"

I actually laugh. "I don't know. Maybe. People think ADHD means I get distracted every time a butterfly goes by, and sure, that happens, but that's not even the half of it. I will actively worry about that butterfly. I will wonder if that butterfly is gonna be okay on the thousands of miles of that species' migration path. Did you know that some butterflies can travel up to a hundred miles in a day? Monarch butterflies can rack up three thousand miles by the time they get where they're going."

Lore smiles.

"Sorry," I say, but I can still feel the laugh in my own voice. "My brain rambles. So I ramble. I know random stuff comes into everyone's heads. I just seem to say it out loud more often."

"Don't be sorry," Lore says. "I like random stuff. In case you haven't noticed."

Lore checks the measurement marks on the syringe, showing me the line we're going for. "Can I ask you something?"

"Yeah," I say, checking the same way Lore does, noting the same line.

"How did you know?" Lore asks. "That you were ready to do this." They double-check for air bubbles.

I try to gauge what kind of answer to give, wondering if Lore's just curious, if it's because they've considered it themself, if they just want to know more about me.

But I don't know why they're asking. So I just tell the truth.

"When you know what you need," I say, "what your body needs, you feel this urgency with it. That's how I knew. Once you know the right thing, every minute you don't do it feels wrong."

"Do you feel different?" Lore asks.

"Yes and no," I say. "I feel a little more like me, if that makes any sense. But that could be because I feel it, or just because I know I'm going in the right direction. It's like when you're lost and then you figure out where you are. Just knowing you're facing the right way changes everything."

I almost ask if Lore knows what I mean. But Lore's smile—slight but open—tells me they do.

Lore shows me how to prime the needle. "We're looking for a bubble." We each gently push on the syringe until a tiny balloon appears at the tip of the needle.

"I see your maelstrom of salamanders," Lore says, waiting for the bubble to slip out of the way for the saline, "and raise you a glory of unicorns."

"Unicorns have a collective noun?" I ask.

"Glory, blessing, or marvel," Lore says. "Maybe there's more. I don't know who decides these things."

"Yeah, who does decide?" I ask. "Has anyone ever seen a group of unicorns?"

"I guess you can decide on a collective noun for just about anything," Lore says. "My mother calls a group of dyslexic people a teeming."

I laugh. "I guess of group of us with ADHD would probably be called a distraction."

"Or a glitter," Lore says.

"I like that better," I say.

Lore holds up their orange. "You ready?"

I nod. "I am the orange."

"According to that"—Lore looks at the instructions— "we want to go in fast, then slow down, check everything, inject slowly, then go back to fast when we pull it out."

*Fast. Slow down. Fast again.* I don't know if Lore even knows they're making patterns for me, but they are, and they stick with me better.

We dart the needles in at the instructed angle, do all the checks, plunger down slow, pull the needle out after.

Seeing someone else have to break down the steps as gradually as I have to makes me feel like maybe I can learn to do this myself. It helps knock down the wall between me and the overwhelming task held in a syringe and a vial.

Lore hands me a prepped Band-Aid.

"Really?" I ask.

"You're still the orange." Lore tapes a Band-Aid over the spot on their orange. I do the same on mine.

Lore looks up and I look toward Lore at the exact same moment. For a second, we're close enough that I can smell the grain of sandpaper. The smell of varnish. The warmth of sawdust.

Lore pulls back like we've static-shocked each other.

I'm staring at them, and I probably look pretty stupid while I'm doing it, and I'm ready for Lore to make some kind of joke about it.

"Nice work, Silvano," Lore says as we put the needles into the sharps container. "You were, in fact, the orange."

"Thank you," I say. "For this."

Lore looks down, smoothing the edges of the Band-Aid. "Anytime."

# LORE

When I dream, the walls around me turn to water. The siding turns translucent, and then transparent. Anyone walking by can see in. Anyone can see everything I tried to leave behind. It all came here with me. It's hiding in unpacked boxes like my shirt.

I wake up blinking into bright light, like the sun's coming through the blinds. But when I open my eyes, I find the room dark. Everything is soaked in the deep violet of dusk, like blue hour.

The glitter jar Bastián gave me throws off comets of light, the water now bright blue, shimmering gold. The glitter swirls like I've just shaken it up. It glistens like sun off new pennies, or tiny points of flame.

As soon as I sit up in bed, I know where I am. The

glitter jar casts fireflies of light, showing me the room. A lamp I know I didn't leave on is now glowing the dark pink of raspberry tea. The walls have turned brilliant green.

If the shift in colors wasn't enough, the stillness in the air is. I can't hear my parents' snoring on the other side of the wall (they like to pretend they don't snore, but they do, practically in unison).

Something taps the outside of the building. It sounds like the echo of a sound I just heard, and realize that's what woke me up, not the light.

I stumble over to the window and slide the pane open.

The tapping is a series of small stones hitting the siding. No, not stones. I catch the tint of each one—amber, green, deep blue. They look like pieces of water-smoothed glass.

Bastián stands on the street outside. They wear jeans that have the wrinkled look of being either slept in or picked up off the floor, with what I'm pretty sure is their favorite hooded sweatshirt. Their hair is sleep-messy. All signs of how fast they left the house.

I lean against the windowsill. I shrug away the nightmare feeling, like it's a dusting of brittle leaves on my shoulders. I don't want Bastián to see any trace of it.

"You've got to get down here," Bastián says.

They seem so awake and alert there's a frequency coming off them. Bastián's so level sometimes and so animated other times, and that may be confusing to someone else, but not to me. I take some things easily and get worked up about others, without a lot of discernable logic. I didn't wince on the drive away from my old street, but when the packing tape gun malfunctioned, I almost threw it against a wall.

An iridescent shimmer makes me look to my left. That's when I see it, the first set of bubbles. They float through the air as slowly as through water, a sheen of color on the surface of each one.

I pull on jeans, zip up a sweatshirt, get my shoes on so fast I'm still pulling them over my heels when I get to the stairs.

I run outside, and stop as soon as I see the dark around me.

The bubbles are everywhere. Not just that one string of them. They drift through the air as gently as stray balloons, each one as big as a fishbowl. And the sheens of color aren't just the iridescence on their surfaces. Each one holds a whirl of color like Bastián's glitter jars.

The world under the lake feels calmer, a universe away from the night the water rushed in.

I step into the middle of the street, reaching my hand out for one of the bubbles.

My fingers barely touch the surface when it breaks open. The currents in the air pull the amber glitter into threads and carry it away.

Then there's nothing between Bastián and me. We

stand in the middle of the street, the asphalt covered in seagrass.

Bastián's face holds so much wonder that I can imagine what they looked like the first time they made a glitter jar. That wonder brightens as we watch the bubbles float up into the purple of the sky. High above us, they break like they're reaching the surface, the glitter spreading out and sticking there in constellations of cotton-candy pink and deep green, pale blue and copper.

Bastián reaches out for one of the bubbles. The surface vanishes, and a twirl of glitter turns to a ribbon in the air, the black of a lace mantilla. I touch another one, and the glitter that spills out is fuchsia that streams through the dark and then vanishes, fast as a minnow. Bastián's fingers meet one that lets out green and blue like a spill of ink.

Above us, more bubbles float upward, making a sky of stars in fire colors and the purple of lavender buds.

With the touch of our fingers, each bubble dissolves, sudden as a hiccup.

I don't realize how close I am to Bastián until a bubble breaks open a second before I touch it. Our fingers brush inside a whirl of silver, the glitter bright as the moon on spider silk.

We don't move our hands.

Bastián touches my arm, cautious and slow. I shiver in a way that makes me feel awake, like when the light turns from blue gray to gold in the morning.

I turn, my cheek so close to Bastián's I can feel their heat.

Everything about Bastián right now stills me. The color of their hair, the night turning it from black brown to true black like it's wet. The dark brown of their widened eyes. The deep acne scar on their left cheek that I thought was a dimple and that I like even more now that I know a little of its story.

Bastián and I are so close their breath touches my lips. Their fingers brush my cheek, cool against the nervous heat on my skin.

It happens so slowly, each of us narrowing the space at the same shivering, hesitating rate, that I can't tell who kisses who. All I know is that they're coming closer, and so am I, and the world around us is such a luminous version of itself that I don't second-guess what I'm doing.

# BASTIÁN

Part of me wants this to be terrible. Part of me wants it to be awkward and stilted, for us to pull away from each other and laugh about how bad it was. Because I've gotten used to liking Lore, but not *liking* Lore.

*Liking* Lore means there's something to break between us. It's not that a friendship between Lore and me couldn't break apart; it could. But this, something like this is so much more fragile. And with everything Lore learns about me, it could get a little more brittle.

Lore knows the side of my ADHD that's unobtrusive enough to fit on index cards and in glitter jars.

Lore doesn't know that when I was a kid, one of my parents or Antonio had to sit with me as I shook that glitter jar to calm down.

Lore doesn't know that I'm so easily distracted that I

had to learn what's common sense to everyone else. I had to build the skill of not absentmindedly walking in front of cars when there isn't a crosswalk.

Lore doesn't know that I forget things even when I care. I will remember the color of nail polish Lore is wearing right now, but it will take three conversations about siblings before I remember whether Lore has any. I will have to explain that this is not because it doesn't matter to me, but because it takes me multiple tries to pin important information in my brain so it sticks.

All that means I kind of want this kiss to be comic-relief-level awful.

But when Lore kisses me, it's everything I've ever noticed about them all at once, each catching the light like the surface of a bubble.

How they pop soda can tabs with one hand in a way that makes me unable to stop looking at their fingers. That chipped green nail polish. The roughness on the backs of their knuckles from the paints and finishes they work with.

The hairpins they slide into the middle of their bra when they wear a bra, the shrug, the *you never know when you might need one.*

How they mostly wear green, orange, yellow, black, gray, brown, the apathy toward typically gendered colors, no blue except jeans. Their fearlessness about all the forms they take, boy, girl, and as many points in between as there are pieces of sea glass on the floor of the lake.

Their soap that smells like green-apple hard candy.

I'm still wondering if I'm making a mistake, kissing this person I've already pulled too far into this world. But the soft, humming feeling inside me, I'm tuning into it like a frequency. That frequency holds one single bright point, the possibility that maybe Lore was right.

Maybe fighting the world under the lake is what's pulling more of it toward the surface. Now that I know something about Lore's brain that they didn't want to tell me, and they know something about mine I didn't want to tell them, the world under the lake isn't rushing above the surface like a storm. It's floating, drifting up, soft as air bubbles. We stop fighting, and the storm settles.

Lore's hand is on my back, brushing the nape of my neck. Lore's mouth takes hold of mine so hard that my next breath feels like coming up for air. And for once, I want to be here, where the world under the lake and world above the surface blur. For right now, instead of this being the space that holds everything I'm afraid of, it's the space that holds everything I want.

We are still, and we are living currents. We are pulsars that appear as single points of blinking light but that hold the bright matter of whole constellations.

This is how the first gleaming wings find us. This is how the butterflies made of lake water swarm around us.

We don't find our way back.

We let our way back find us.

# LORE

o you want to tell me about what happened at your last school?" Amanda the Learning Specialist asks.

The question checks me in the sternum. We were just talking about study strategies, audiobooks, learning accommodations. How did we get here? What turn did I miss?

"I made a mistake," I say. "I want to move past it. The rest of it doesn't really matter, does it?"

Amanda the Learning Specialist looks at me for a long time, like she wants to make sure I'm done talking. "Does that feel true?"

"What do you mean does it feel true?" I ask.

"Does that feel like the story you want to tell?" Amanda the Learning Specialist asks.

I want to tell her that it's the only story anyone will ever want. I'm brown, and trans, and I have a learning disability. My sheer existence is as much nuance as I get to have. Who I am uses up all the space the world is willing to give me, and even that, I have to fight to keep open. I am already a living confrontation. My story doesn't get to be complicated.

"It's all there is," I say. "That's it."

Amanda the Learning Specialist nods.

After a minute she asks, "Did you bring your favorite book?"

"No." I probably overact the expression meant to say *I forgot and am just now remembering.* I can tell I've overdone it so much I might as well have snapped my fingers and added a *darn it all.* "Sorry."

"Did you bring your workbook?" Amanda the Learning Specialist asks.

"I left it on the kitchen counter," I say.

I answered that way too fast for this to be a believable lie.

I try to save it.

"I even told myself to grab it on the way out," I say, "and then I just forgot."

Amanda the Learning Specialist doesn't look like she believes it. I'm hoping she forgets entirely that she asked me to handwrite in the spiral-bound workbook. I know what my handwriting looks like. It's messy, inconsistent, chaotic. It tilts in all different directions. I don't think it'll encourage Amanda the Learning Specialist to give a glowing report.

"Sorry about that," I say.

Amanda the Learning Specialist sounds neither annoyed nor dissuaded when she says, "Bring them next time."

My hands find the glitter jar in my bag. When Amanda the Learning Specialist asks me about it, I tell her. I take the opening to slip in how I've already made friends in my new town. I give her what she needs to write down that I'm *pleasant*, that I *make friends easily*, that I am *an absolute delight*.

I tell her about Bastián, about their ADHD. I tell her how I probably wouldn't have guessed if they hadn't told me, and I don't realize why I'm saying that until a minute later. I'm hoping Amanda the Learning Specialist will tell me no one would ever guess that I'm dyslexic.

She doesn't.

"You know those are also called calming jars, right?" she says. "They help with emotional regulation."

I turn it so the sparkles tumble over themselves.

"Did you know ADHD and dyslexia have something in common?" Amanda the Learning Specialist asks.

I shake my head.

I shake the glitter jar.

"They both affect executive functioning," she says. "Working memory. Emotional regulation. Problem solving."

I am about to ask, *What are you saying, Amanda—that if I'd had a glitter jar I wouldn't have become the kid who beat the shit out of someone? That all this could have been avoided with some sparkles?*

For a minute, I'm back in elementary school, with adults telling me to say the alphabet backward to calm myself down. I can still feel the rage building like pressure in my shoulders. If you ever want to make someone dyslexic who's angry even angrier, tell them to say the alphabet backward.

I watch only the gold glitter, then only the green, like the flashes on the horizon right before the sun goes down.

"Does your friend know?" Amanda the Learning Specialist asks.

"About what?" I ask.

"That you're dyslexic," Amanda the Learning Specialist says.

"Yeah," I say. "Of course." As though I told Bastián the first time we met, as though I just dropped it into conversation right after my name and pronouns.

"Do they know what happened?" she asks.

I shake my head.

I shake the glitter jar.

"You don't have to tell them," Amanda the Learning Specialist says. "You don't have to tell anyone."

"I know," I say.

"But if you ever decide to," she says, "you can. It's not something you have to hide."

I mean to nod, but because I'm still shaking the glitter jar, I shake my head too.

I believe that Amanda the Learning Specialist believes what she's saying.

Amanda the Learning Specialist is also white. And Bastián's friends, the ones who are white and the ones who aren't, all qualify as who adults would call Nice Kids. Abril in her floral skirts and the posture that's both open and upright, like a ballet teacher for little kids. Maddie with her wide, curious eyes and welcoming smile and unbitten nails. Bastián with their ironed work khakis and deferential nod to anyone older. They are all the definition of Nice Kids. Not Troubled. Not Aggressive. Not all the things someone, and then everyone, will call me if they know *what happened*, which is Amanda-the-Learning-Specialist code for *what I did*.

When I leave the session with Amanda the Learning Specialist, my shoulder blades flinch with the sense that someone is following me. Every set of strangers' footsteps behind me sounds like ones I know. They're not. I know that. But even though I know that, the memory is so sharp that I can hear those guys trying to get me to look back, how they'll roar with satisfaction if I do.

I don't look back. I don't fall into the memory of being so scared that I have to check over my shoulder.

I wait for the bus. I get on. I don't look at anyone. But in the rattling of the bus engine, I hear them imitating me in fourth grade, mocking the stuttering, uncertain noises I made when I tried to read, when the teacher told me to *sound it out, just sound it out.* I hear them imitating me for years after, and me learning to ignore it.

I feel the sting of their glares when they stop getting the reaction they want.

The sound twists and spins. It pitches higher. The frequency through my chest, the high laugh I've been hearing at home. It's back, and now it's following me. It won't let me go. It's even louder now, noise flaring inside my brain.

When the bus stops, I'm almost running to get off. But the second I'm off, I'm facing darkness. A minute ago the sky was pale through the bus windows, washed out by clouds. Now it's the blue of deep water, tinted green and purple at the edges.

Everywhere there's usually brush is seagrass. Everywhere there's usually rocks there are different colors of stones. No. Sea glass, polished pieces of cobalt and beer-bottle green, frosted clear glass, the gray green and pale amber of old wine bottles.

I look down the road, but the bus is already gone. All I can hear is the last far-off whir of the engine, and then the rising echo of that laugh.

"What do you want?" I shout into the noise. The laugh wrings out my brain, so I scream back at it. "What do you want from me?"

But the sky folds away my voice, and it vanishes. A sound somewhere between air crashing into air and water crashing into water makes me turn my head.

Over where the lake would be—I can't see from here if the lake is water or seagrass right now—color shifts and tumbles. It looks like clouds, or how waves look from underwater when they break, the crashing and billowing foam.

The clouds shift colors, the storm coming in fast.

# BASTIÁN

Sometimes, ADHD feels like trying to get a fitted sheet on a bed when the sheet's a little too small. I get one corner on, another flies off. I figure things out at school, but tap out my brain so much I don't want to talk to anyone when I get home. I show up everywhere forty-five minutes early (because it's either that or twenty minutes late), then forget to screw the top back on my water bottle before I shove it into my backpack.

Today, it means deciding, in the middle of folding my laundry, that it's absolutely time to organize my desk drawer.

What happens when I get lost in doing something—whether it's this, or painting alebrijes—they call it hyper-focus.

Hyperfocus. It's why, when I look up, I have no idea how long I've been in this version of my room.

Hyperfocus. It's what makes me startle when I notice the walls are the color of wet cilantro. The glitter jars are luminescent as deep-sea jellyfish.

People who don't have brains like mine might not panic as fast as I do, or as often. But getting startled out of hyperfocus feels like being shaken out of sleepwalking. Which is why I run into the hall, looking for Mom and Mamá, before remembering that they're never in this version of our house, or this version of the world.

Every time I move, the echo of a memory finds me. When I look back at my desk, I remember crawling under it when I read take-home test directions for the third time and couldn't parse them. I pass the closet I hid in because Mom and Mamá were having Nochebuena at our house, and it was too many voices, too many people talking at me, too many people I knew and didn't know trying to touch my hair or my face.

I pick up a phone, but instead of a dial tone, it's the sound of rushing water, a whole lake of it. I pick up the one in the kitchen, and the noise is a storm.

I throw open doors, still looking for Mom or Mamá. At the back of my mind, I know they're not here. I know throwing open doors isn't going to help me.

I open a hall closet, and paint spools through the air. I

check the bathroom, and pieces of sea glass swirl around the bathtub drain in marigold-orange water. I check the kitchen.

A line of cookbooks sit glowing on a shelf, spines illuminated. One wings through the air and opens. Glaringly white pages tear out of it, a few at a time. My stomach kicks when I recognize it, the cookbook I ripped into pieces when I couldn't follow a recipe, when I tried it and it turned out so spectacularly wrong I couldn't see the point of trying.

Cups I haven't seen in years show up on the counters, ones I broke because I was clumsy, or because I was so desperate to be helpful that I carried too many at a time, or because I was so distracted I forgot I had a cup in one hand.

Light illuminates their rims, like they're holding neon. But when I come closer, they tilt off the edges. One by one, they shatter on the floor, sending me stumbling back.

From the closet where paint is swirling through the air comes a faint echo. I hear the far-off sound of myself screaming when I was so overwhelmed all I could do was sit in the dark. I hadn't yet learned to tell anyone what I needed, or even learned to know what I needed. So I just screamed into the hems of coats, the heavy fabric muffling the sound as I tried to make my brain quiet.

It's all coming to the surface, everything I sent down with the alebrijes. Outside the window, I see them swimming up near the watery moon. Yellow and red branches sway against the night.

The weather in my brain goes past heat or searing light. It's parched and wind-thrown. It's wildfire weather, the kind that can take a single spark and spread it through my brain. Everything gets leveled. Every time I try to find a place solid enough to get my footing, it turns to ash and crumbles underneath me. All the water in the world under the lake gathers and buckles into the shape of flames.

A door hinge whines.

The front door opens. Not like anyone's opening it. More like it's shrugging open.

"Bastián." Lore runs into the house.

I back up. "You can't be here."

Lore stops just inside.

I keep backing up. "You can't be here."

My shoulder hits a door frame. A column of pain goes through me.

Lore says my name again.

As the pain of hitting my shoulder blade dulls, I think of a word we learned in physics. *Impulse.* Not *impulse* as in *impulsive.* Impulse as in the mathematical, physical concept.

Force divided by time. Hitting a wall hurts more than leaning against it because of how fast it happens. Slamming into a sidewalk damages you so much more than jumping into a pile of leaves because the first one will stop you cold in a split second, while the leaves absorb your momentum gradually, slowing you down.

Impulse: The same force has more of an impact on you the faster it happens.

And Lore is about to know everything about me all at once. Too fast, so the impulse will hit hard enough to break whatever exists between me and them.

If Lore sees these pieces of myself I've left behind—in the broken cups, the torn pages, my hands gripping the closet shut, my low, raw screams caught in the cracks between tiles—they'll see the worst of what living in my brain looks like. And all of that will take up more space than anything Lore or anyone else likes about me.

Maybe, eventually, if Lore knew me enough to know enough good things about me, they could take the impact of all this. But they don't know that much good, nowhere near.

"Are you okay to be touched right now?" Lore asks.

The inside of me feels like a knot most of the time. So when it loosens, like it does now, that's the strange thing, like I'm coming apart. And in that unknotting, something else comes together.

Lore listened, not just to what I told them but what I didn't. I asked if hugs were okay with them because I wished people had asked me.

Lore isn't touching me unless I say okay.

"Yes," I say.

"Is there anywhere you don't want me to touch you right now?" Lore asks, slow, careful.

"No," I say, fast as darting the needle into the orange.

Lore brushes pieces of hair out of my face, their fingers cool against my skin.

"I'm not gonna pretend I've never wished my brain was different," Lore says. "I've wished it more times than I could ever tell you. But if it was, I might not understand the way my mom thinks as much as I do. I might not have learned to read by hearing my dad read to me, so we wouldn't have read together as much."

Lore rests their forehead against mine in a way that makes me shut my eyes.

"Sometimes you can't separate the hard things from the good things," Lore whispers.

The door hinge whines again.

Lore and I both open our eyes.

A current of air eases the front door open wider, and new sound comes in.

# LORE

The noise starts in the trees. Then it echoes off the sky that looks like clouds or water breaking into water.

But this isn't a storm, or a laugh. It's the static of something too far away to understand.

Slowly, like tuning the dial of an old radio, the noise pulls into words. Each word I recognize gives the charge of something familiar in an unfamiliar context. A crow that's gotten inside the post office. An old picture of my mother, age five, climbing the tree in my abuela's backyard.

*Sound it out. Just sound it out.* The same words echo in a dozen voices, some frustrated, some laughing, some taunting.

My heart catches, and goes still.

Everything I tried not to bring with me when my family had to move, everything I never wanted anyone else to know, it's humming out of the sidewalks and the blades of underwater grass coating the street.

I don't just remember it. I'm inside it.

I'm small, and a teacher who didn't like me even before she found out how I read is telling me, in increasingly frustrated repetitions, to *sound it out, just sound it out.* And I cannot force what she's asking of me because my brain will not do it. My brain will not give my mouth the tentative but promising sounds other kids are making. The *b* before *blue.* The almost-hum of *y* before *yellow.* The long pause on the *o* of *orange* and thickening emphasis on the last sound.

I cannot say the words on the page, not the way she wants. I know them. I can sight-read them. But I cannot sound them out. I cannot bridge the words I know by heart and the sounds they break down into.

Instead, my brain, my mouth, form only one refrain— *I'm stupid, I'm stupid, I'm stupid.* It gets hot on my tongue, and to keep myself from screaming it, I grit my teeth so hard I think I might crack a molar.

I walk out the front door, not because I want to meet everything outside, but because I have to stand between all of it and Bastián. I have to stop it from coming inside.

"Lore," Bastián says, apprehension tinting their voice.

"Stay here," I say, the words as hard and steady as I can make them.

I can't do anything about what Bastián remembers from their own life and wishes they didn't. But I can stop this, because it's not here for Bastián. It's here for me.

If I stand at the sidewalk, maybe that'll be as far as it gets. If I can stop it, none of it will find its way into Bastián's house.

When I get outside, years of voices in hallways find me, all of them saying *Why don't you sound it out?* They say it every time they pass me. They imitate my stuttering breaths when I try not to cry during reading time.

I throw back at them things I hear my parents say. *Why don't you come up with some new material?* Or, *Oh yeah, that's original.* I learn to shrug it off, same as the comments about my lunch, how I bring food they don't know in repurposed plastic containers, instead of the juice boxes and individually wrapped cookies that are currency in grade school.

I pretend none of it touches me. I continually hold my jaw in that clench. Later, this will help me be a boy, the practice sharpening the angles in my face.

When I tell adults about them making fun of me in the halls, the adults tell me that if I ignore them, they'll ignore me. When that doesn't work, I tell them again. They tell me that I should learn to laugh with them, that if I learn to laugh at myself, to not take myself so seriously, I might find myself making some new friends.

So I do. When they laugh at me, I force a laugh, even with my jaw still tight. And at first it works. They look at me like someone's little brother they have greater affection for because of how easy I am to mess with. They laugh at me. I laugh at me. And out of our agreement over how easy I am to make fun of, a truce emerges.

But then there's the spelling bee, my blank horror at the word *veterinarian*. There's the library book in my backpack, one they think I'm too old for. There's the fact of us getting older, our bodies changing enough that everything turns, that old jokes now have the new, thrilling edge of being spoken in deeper voices or from greater heights.

They start taunting me with *sound it out* again, because I still cannot sound it out. This is evident in the face of archaic words that show up in English class and the unfamiliar terms in our science textbooks.

This time, I do not laugh. I cannot laugh. My jaw has grown so tight I can't do it.

I stop laughing. With each cue they give me to laugh, each time I don't laugh, they grow increasingly offended at this silent suggestion that their jokes are not funny.

So the next time they tell me to *sound it out*, they grab at my sleeves, the edges of my jacket, to make sure I can't just keep walking. And something in my brain begins to splinter.

I tell other adults how if they're in a hallway, I can't get past them. When I get caught cutting behind the school to avoid them, I say why.

The adults ask why I would ever tell such awful lies about the sons of such nice families.

I don't think there's always one moment you realize racism is a thing that lives and breathes instead of something in history books, because really, you know it your whole life. You know it in the color of dolls on shelves, the color of villains on TV.

But you make excuses for the world. Another channel must have the brown-skinned heroes. The brown dolls must be somewhere else.

This is the moment I know for sure, though, that it isn't all some big misunderstanding, that it isn't a coincidence that the bad guys in movies have darker skin and eyes and hair than the good guys. That's when I know it's that way because someone—or really, a lot of someones—not only made it that way but have been keeping it that way ever since.

I can't tell you why I do what I do in the particular moment I do it.

Maybe the brittle part of my brain that's been cracking apart finally breaks into splinters. Maybe it's that after years of something you grit your teeth trying to take, there's a moment you just can't anymore. Your teeth slip. You bite the inside of your cheek. Or your jaw gets tired of clenching down that hard.

Maybe it's that Merritt Harnish grabs my shirt so hard that he gets not just my shirt but the edge of my binder. His grip on both layers is so tight I can feel the right side of my chest moving in the front. When he lets it go, it snaps back, and I can feel the pain going through my rib cage.

So I turn around.

I hit him hard enough to give him an instant nosebleed. He'll feel the pain of the impact later, but right now, the adrenaline comes fast enough that all he feels is the shock of it.

That's the part everyone will talk about first.

Merritt grabs me by the collar.

I'll never know if I'm right, but in this moment, I think he's remembering Jilly Uhlenbruck watching on that field trip, laughing at him like he's laughed at me for years. Right now, that moment and this moment are the same. They take up one point in space.

I hit him again.

He slams me into a wall hard enough that my temple will be some shade of purple or blue or sickly yellow for the next two weeks. Pain spins through my head, knocking off more splinters.

He reaches to grab my shirt again.

I bring my knee up into his crotch.

The sound I rip out of him draws a crowd.

He's still stumbling through the pain when a new round of rage puffs him back up. I don't expect him to come back from it that fast. So when he rushes at me, he gets me down on the concrete.

He draws back a fist, getting the momentum to send it into my cheek or my temple.

The muscles in my jaw want to brace, to wince. My eyes want to shut so I can go somewhere else until he's done bloodying up my face.

But I keep my eyes open.

I don't turn away.

I make him look at me.

I stare up at him so that he can see all of the irises, dark and blazing enough to bore into him. I make him see all of the brown. I make him see so much of a color he hates.

He drops his fist.

Everyone watching thinks it's because, right then, the teachers are rushing in to break it up.

But a split second before the teachers' voices find us, I see something in Merritt Harnish's face. A shift. Like he's remembering himself.

It's fast, but in that split second, I see the truth of him.

He doesn't hate me because I fought back.

He doesn't even hate me because I'm too stupid to *sound it out*.

He hates me because, for a second, I made him see me as a boy. I got him to fight me like a boy, and to him, that humiliation is unforgivable.

I only see it for a second, his horror at what I have made him do. It's the only time I will see it. In another half second, it will turn to rage. Then that rage will get stretched into a roiling disgust that he has to share a hallway, a school, a city, with me.

The weeks after are a cycle of ice packs, meetings with school administrators, debates about the length of my suspension.

Merritt's friends follow me home, saying they hope I enjoy watching my ass because I'll get to do a lot of it. They offer what they call friendly advice, telling me if they were me they wouldn't sleep until graduation.

They don't do anything to me. That's not the point. The point is that they like me not knowing if or when they might.

Then comes my parents' late-night conversations, ones they think I can't hear. They talk about moving, their fears that if we stay, I'll come home beaten up or broken. Something that happened in the middle of the school year isn't going away, it's getting worse.

"Lore." Bastián's voice slices through the noise of what I remember.

I startle and turn around. I stumble deeper into the marine grass.

No. Bastián can't be out here. They can't be in this current of noise rushing over me like water. They can't have heard everything, from every imitated syllable to Merritt

Harnish's friends telling me why I should consider myself lucky, speaking the words that still cling to the back of my shirt. *The only reason his family isn't going after your ass is because you're a girl.*

I know Bastián's heard it, everything that the world under the lake is throwing back at me. I can tell by how they stare, mouth slack with something that would look like empathy if I didn't know what they're probably thinking.

They may not know everything. They may not know how and why it happened. But they heard enough.

Bastián doesn't make mistakes like I do. Bastián is the kind of person who folds their pajamas into a neat square and sets them under their pillow. I am the kind of person who drops my clothes on the floor so fast my mother makes jokes about me being raptured.

Bastián would never do what I did. They may be in constant fights with their own brain, but they'd never lose one that disastrously.

Before me, the world under the lake was strange and disconcerting but beautiful. What I brought in is sharp and violent. It's not a refracted moon or a lapping tide. It's rushing water and crashing furniture. I have not only dragged the worst of myself into what was supposed to be my new life here, I have brought the worst of myself into the secret landscape Bastián shared with me.

The clouds let out a noise between thunder and crashing waves.

When I leave, Bastián calls my name.

But I don't turn around.

I look for anything that could be one of the lake's seiches, layers of water slipping out farther into the dark.

I want the purple night to turn deep blue. I want the underwater grass filling the street to go back to asphalt. I want the bright colors to fade from the trees.

But I get all the way home, and none of it's turned back.

I stand on the sidewalk.

The building doesn't look right. The walls are thinning out, the wood becoming so threadbare I can see through it in places. But instead of the wood looking brittle and splintered, it looks wet and slick.

The walls of the building are turning to water. They're turning translucent in places, showing flashes of what's inside. Patches go transparent and then solid again. Colors swim over the surface like a bubble before it pops.

The shiver of a laugh slides toward me. It streams out through the walls, rippling the water. It crawls over my skin. It settles onto my own tongue. It vibrates in my throat and lungs.

The horror of understanding blooms in my chest.

Of course I didn't recognize this laugh.

It's not my real laugh. It's not the familiar one I

inherited from my mother. It's not even my fake laugh, the one I give when my youngest primos try to tell jokes and mess up the punch lines.

This is my scared laugh. It's the one I forced when adults told me to laugh along with Merritt and his friends. It's the halting, nervous laugh I willed out of myself even when my throat didn't want to give it up.

The laugh that's haunted me isn't some unknown voice, or even Merritt's or his friends'. It's the noise I had to make to survive, but that never really belonged to me. That sound is a ghost outside me.

Abril's words come back to me.

*It's always been a house with a lot of feelings.*

It took mine into its very walls.

I try to slow down my breathing. I try to shove everything that's gotten loose back into the small, brittle space inside my chest.

But it won't stay. Even when the seiche skims over the sidewalk and takes me back to the world I know, I can't shove it all back down. The frequency of my own forgotten laugh rings through my brain. It's the trembling reminder that I made so many mistakes before I threw my fist at Merritt Harnish.

# BASTIÁN

I want to tell Lore that it doesn't matter. Well, not that it doesn't matter. Of course it does. It will never not matter. Whatever happened is a jagged wound in Lore. I could see it in their face and the way their stance changed. I could feel their fear vibrating through the air.

I couldn't make enough sense of all that noise to know exactly what happened. But I do know that anyone who told Lore to *sound it out* never deserved them.

The next morning, as I'm restocking printer paper, I hold on to one possibility: If I don't know everything about what happened to Lore, maybe Lore doesn't know everything about me either.

I mail a postcard to my brother, a painting of that kind of spiral shell my brain feels like right now, all those curves and chambers that sound bounces around in. And as though he can feel it dropping into the mailbox, as soon as I get home, he calls.

"The dogs miss you," Antonio says. "And Michelle's convinced you don't like her."

"I do so like her," I say.

"They say they do so like you," Antonio yells in a way that sounds like it's across the room.

"Of course they do," I hear Michelle yell back. "I'm delightful. If they don't like anyone, it's definitely you."

"Come on." Antonio's talking to me again. "We'll take over the whole kitchen. Papier-mâché everywhere. We'll have a house full of alebrijes by the time we're done."

"I started T," I blurt out.

I don't even realize I'm thinking of saying it until I already have.

"And?" Antonio asks.

"And what?" I ask.

"How do you feel?" he asks.

"I've only had one dose," I say. "I don't feel much yet. I guess I feel a little more like me. But that could be in my head."

"Feeling more like you *is* in your head," Antonio says. "You got to feel it there before you feel it everywhere else, right?"

I have no idea. Sometimes it starts in the core of my body, the feeling of my binder holding me in. Sometimes it's my hands, doing something that keeps my brain still.

Right now, it's the knot loosening in my chest.

"So this is why you've been avoiding me?" Antonio asks.

Even before I realized I was trans, I always studied my brother, the way he moves his body and his hands, the way he laughs, the way he puts on a jacket or sits in a chair. I started wearing a watch because Antonio wore one. But now that I'm looking toward what the testosterone will make of my body, I'm thinking even more about what I might make of myself. While it's doing its work of slightly rearranging my cells, I'm thinking about the kind of boy I want to be, and that looks a lot like my brother.

So is he going to think I'm trying to imitate him (especially since sometimes I am)? Is he going to shudder if my face looks like his, or if my voice ends up sounding too much like his?

"Kind of," I say.

"Then don't," Antonio says. "I'm proud of you for doing what's gonna make you feel like you."

The knot of my heart unclenches a little more. Antonio has always been somewhere between older brother and uncle. So when he sees me, it's like getting seen twice. The impact, the spectacular impulse of it, is as strong as when Mom and Mamá started using my pronouns like it was nothing, like it was easy because it was right.

"What's the rest of it?" Antonio asks.

"The rest of what?" I ask.

"You said starting T is *kind of* why you've been avoiding me," Antonio says. "What's the rest?"

I look at the line of alebrijes crowding my desk.

I want to tell Lore that what I heard, what the world under the lake threw back at Lore, doesn't change anything to me. I want to tell them I don't care. Anything that happened may be part of Lore, but it's not them.

Except that, when it comes to myself, I don't really believe that. And if I don't believe there's nothing to be ashamed of, how can Lore?

# BASTIÁN

**T**his time, I don't wait for the world under the lake to come above the surface. I go down to the water, passing the LAKELORE sign that's so weathered and faded the letters barely show.

I climb down to the inlet. I wait for the water to break into a swarm of blue-green and silver wings, showing me the path underneath.

The alebrijes drift through the dark, a few coming slightly forward again, trying to get me to follow them.

This time, I do. If this is what they want, if there's any chance that they're coming above the surface trying to find me, this is the only move I have left.

I follow the pieces of lit-up sea glass. The rounds of yellow and green and blue get thicker on the ground as they lead me in.

The farther I go, the more the ground squishes under my feet. I remember this, the wet, soft moss, like I'm walking on the bottom of a pond.

My heart pulls back into a knot. Harder than a knot. It's a dense thing with a quasar's gravity. It pulls me back toward being the boy I was years ago, who didn't know how to live with my own brain.

As I go farther down, the ground breaks apart and rises up. Fallen trees crowd patches of the lake bed, like a waterlogged forest. Pieces of what look like wrecked boats catch under the trunks, the lacquered wood scratched. The hull of a coble boat is so rusted over I can barely see the paint.

I dodge around the broken wood, the glow of amber sea glass guiding me forward.

From the dark, the hot glow of live ash winks at me. The flashes come in pairs, the stares of alebrijes with eyes like meteors. To anyone else, those points of smoldering light might seem threatening, a warning. But to me, they're as familiar as the walls of my room, alebrijes whose eyes I made out of tiny plastic jewels or sequins that turned to embers when they came to life.

I know what's waiting for me here. Echoes of me hiding in closets, lying on the floor with my hands over my eyes, screaming if someone tried to move me or touch me.

An alebrije owl flies past, feathers wearing a sprinkling of leaf-green scales. An octopus with flames for tentacles crosses a far corner of the dark. An ocelot with the wings of a monarch butterfly looks at me, eyes hot and glittering.

Water thyme sways alongside the green ribbons of wild water celery. Yellow and pale purple flowers dot the star grass. And among the boats and underwater trees are things I didn't know were here.

The couple of refrigerators could have just ended up down here—a lot of things end up on the bottom of a lake. Except one is deep green and another is red violet, and they look like dyed-bright versions of the fridges I've climbed on at home, at Antonio's old apartment, at Antonio and Michelle's house.

Pinned under pieces of sea glass are leaves of paper with my handwriting on them. Index cards, in every color.

Glitter jars rest in beds of seagrass, gathering light and throwing it back in tiny rainbows.

The world under the lake isn't just holding the parts of myself and my history that I don't want to think about.

It's holding the ways I adapted, and lived.

*Sometimes you can't separate the hard things from the good things.*

I hear the words the way Lore said them. I hear them as I remember their hair in two braids, a gray sweatshirt, the pull of their heart as strong and whirling as the spin of a planet.

This place holds not only reminders of when I gripped the windowsill so hard it left splinters in my palms, or when I couldn't filter out the noise in the halls at school. It holds the way I took what my brain threw at me, and how I turned it over, wearing down the broken edges until they were sea glass.

I feel in my hands, in the tension in my knuckles, how hard I've tried. I shove all of this down, and then, like a balloon, it bobs up above the surface. It's as unbothered by my effort as I am drained by it. I didn't realize how tired all this was making me. Not just the effort it takes me to function, but the effort it takes to make it look like it's not effort. Trying to act like it doesn't cost me anything is costing me more than I have.

I am so tired of trying to keep the buoy of how my brain works under the water, of how, every time, I'm breaking my own heart hoping it stays there.

# LORE

f I could will myself to laugh when I didn't want to, why can't I do this?

What Amanda the Learning Specialist tells my new school will depend in part on this stupid workbook. I keep thinking the same words over and over. *Just fill it out. Just write it in.* But that twists, fast, into *Sound it out.*

Shards of color spill across my room.

I check the glitter jar Bastián made me, but the sun's not hitting it.

I follow where the pieces of light are coming from, toward the window.

The sun is hitting a glitter jar down on the sidewalk, lighting up the deep lilac of the water and bouncing off the pieces of glitter. It's so bright that it takes me a second to see Bastián holding it.

I set my back against the wall.

The center of my heart spins and glows, while the bristling in my shoulder blades wants me to stay up here until Bastián leaves. Maybe even until Bastián graduates.

But the heat at the center of my heart sends light down to my fingers. I reach for the doorknob.

I go downstairs.

I meet Bastián on the sidewalk.

Bastián hands me the glitter jar. "I thought maybe you could use another one."

"If you have questions about what happened," I say, "I don't want to answer them."

"I don't," Bastián says.

The purple light of the glitter jar fills my hands.

"Please," Bastián says. "Just come with me, okay?"

Even with the flare of light behind them, I can see Bastián's face enough to know they mean this. They're not picking apart what they heard, or trying to find out more than they already know.

So I go with them.

As we pass the LAKELORE sign, the letters look even less visible than before, the blowing dust sanding them off.

We stand at the edge of the lake.

Bastián stares out at the water. "I never thought someone would know all of me and accept all of me. And I'm not gonna tell you that you're the first one who ever did that, because you're not. My family, my friends, they've been doing that this whole time. I just thought that the only reason they did is because I was keeping the difficult parts of me somewhere else."

As Bastián's talking, the water flickers open in a whirl of silver and blue.

I look at them. "Are you sure about this?"

Bastián nods, the wind off the water blowing their hair into their eyes. "Trust me, okay?"

A little at a time, like an old bulb warming up, the way in front of us lights up the dark.

The air around us drifts in ribbons, luminescent. It takes me a minute to realize, to remember, that it's not just the air. There are stands of kelp around us, wavering like we're underwater. They've grown thicker since the last time I saw them. With each ripple of movement, the leaves flash from moss green to pale purple.

An alebrije flies past, with the hard shell of an armadillo body, the sharp blue-green of dragonfly wings, the marigold-orange of a forked tongue.

Since I found Bastián again, I've known this place was real, and not something I imagined. But seeing it up close like this, it becomes a kind of true it's never been until now. The landscape glows against the dark, bare branches of underwater trees turning orange and fuchsia at the edges. Broken boats and a yellow refrigerator list to the side. Paper flutters like wings.

Bastián stops, olive and yellow-green sea glass around

our feet. "When you came back, I remembered that sometimes people see me. All of me. And that was terrifying. You woke up that feeling in me of being seen, and I didn't like it because I'd forgotten how much I need it."

Something about Bastián's face is different. Everything I've memorized is still there. The brown of their skin and hair and eyes. The shape of their brow bone, the right eyebrow curving a little more than the left. But they seem clearer, in focus.

"And now I'm just talking without thinking, and I didn't realize that I still know how to do that without it going wrong." Bastián's laugh sounds nervous but not scared. "So I'm gonna tell you what you told me because I really needed to hear it. And I'm wondering if you do too." Bastián breathes out. "You can't separate everything hard from everything beautiful."

My heart feels soft as the oranges we practiced with.

I can't meet Bastián where they are. What they need has just as much weight and gravity as what I need, but it's a universe away. For me, none of this is about embracing my brain the way it is, or about understanding that dyslexia doesn't make me stupid. My mother's existence taught me that dyslexia doesn't make anyone stupid. My mother has decades of items that won't match up, inventory systems that will never completely reconcile words heard with words written out, but she can sketch a map of a town she's been to one time, to scale, in a few minutes.

None of this is about my dyslexia. It's not about why I can't *sound it out*.

This is about the decisions I made when I couldn't hear *Sound it out* one more taunting time.

This isn't about what I am. This is about what I did. This is about a kind of stupid I was that had nothing to do with my dyslexia.

It's not that I ever thought I could leave my dyslexia behind. But I do need to leave behind everything I did. And I can't do that while this boy is looking at me knowing what they know.

I make sure I don't look at Bastián's mouth, so I won't remember how it felt on mine, so I can lie.

"I don't feel about you the way I think you feel about me," I say.

Bastián flinches, but recovers fast. "That's okay," they say. "I'm not asking you to feel a certain way about me. I just want to know you, if you want that."

I step back, knocked off balance by how well Bastián takes this. I'm used to boys feeling entitled to you after they kiss you, or as soon as they want to. I'm not used to boys who say *That's okay* when you tell them you've had as much of them as you want.

I tense my fallen, bruised orange of a heart.

I tell an even more spectacular lie.

"I don't want to be friends," I say.

Bastián looks so pained I almost tell them that I don't

mean it. But I can't go further with this boy who knows this much about me, not even as friends. I can't go deeper into this world that knows so much about their secrets and mine.

"Okay," Bastián says, pulling it together so hard I can see them straightening their body. "I understand."

Bastián doesn't look at me. They nod, tracing the toe of their shoe between pieces of sea glass.

*Come on*, I want to yell at them. *Be an asshole. Tell me I owe you something. Get angry about this. Give me something that lets me write you off as not worth knowing.*

But nothing.

If I stay for a few more seconds, Bastián will make themself look up at me, and the pain in their eyes might break me apart. It wouldn't even take that much. The sight of Bastián's fingers on their watchband, the fidgeting rhythm of turning it on their wrist, that would be enough to splinter me into pieces.

So I go back the way we came, following the illuminated green and brown of the path. I follow the rounded glass, tinted and frosted by the wear of water. And as I walk, I feel something like ribbons of kelp falling away from me, like it's not just Bastián letting me go, but the world under the lake.

# BASTIÁN

When Lore walks away, I can almost see it, how the threads connecting them to the world under the lake snap and fall. It looks like faint strands of light against the dark, so delicate they may or may not be there.

Maybe that's why it doesn't surprise me when the world under the lake doesn't come above the surface that night, because it's let go of Lore. Or it could be because I'm not fighting it anymore. I went back. It's no longer the place that holds everything I want to keep at a distance. I went back for all those parts of me, so all those parts of me don't have to come looking for me anymore.

# LORE

fight it off, that flinchy, pre-crying feeling. I tense every muscle I can feel. I put everything into my hands. I sand down more chairs. I rub the grain of the paper over the old wood, seeing but not feeling how raw it's leaving my knuckles.

It's not just that I told Bastián I didn't want them, not like that. It's that Bastián and their world can pull me back toward my old life, and I can't let that happen.

So now I'm not just hiding from Bastián, I'm hiding from their friends who were becoming my friends too. The more I'm around them, the more I'll see Bastián.

Sweat slicks my lower back and soaks a patch of my binder. My knees ache from kneeling on the concrete, the shins of my jeans wearing down.

I spin past thinking about Bastián, past thinking about their friends. I think about my mom and dad, and the books they held open, not minding how often I looked over their shoulders. Sometimes my father would be reading a book just for him—Greek myths, or the history of farming in the Andes—and I would climb on the back of the sofa and stare at the page. He would start reading out loud like it was nothing, like he wasn't even doing it for me, even though I was perched on the edge of the sofa, trying to memorize the words as he read them.

My father shared those rare quiet hours with a child who was both drawn to books and terrified by them.

And my mother. She read out loud to me even when she was still stumbling over words she had never seen in print, or hadn't seen enough times to match up how they sound.

They did all that for me, and I still wrecked everything.

I go harder at my work, the sound of sandpaper on wood crowding out what I don't want to think about. This is one thing I can do right. I failed when I threw that first punch. I failed when we had to move. Then I failed at keeping what happened from following me. Even the walls here knew it. So it's only a matter of time until I fail at the chance my parents wanted me to have here.

But this, the wood under my hands, this is my chance

to do something good. I can clean and sand and varnish and paint until I have something more to offer than this handful of failures.

"Lore," I hear in my mother's voice, but she sounds far away.

I keep sanding, covering more area faster, trying to make the brushing, scraping noises sound less like Merritt Harnish's rasping laugh and more like the grain of the paper on wood.

"Lore," my mother's voice says again.

I don't notice the backs of my hands are splitting open until a thread of blood stains the sandpaper.

"Lore."

My mother kneels in front of me. Her work apron brushes the floor.

She eases the sandpaper from my trembling fingers.

"You can stop," she whispers.

I shake my head, refusing to sniffle, trying to tell her I'm good, I can keep going. It's just the dust making me fuzzy.

She holds my hands. "Whatever you're doing, whatever you've been trying to do since we got here." She dips her head to catch my eye. "You can stop now."

That's how it happens, the thing I decided I wouldn't do.

I break apart.

I splinter like brittle wood.

I cry as a boy.

# BASTIÁN

amá watches me start the kettle.

Intently.

"Everything okay?" I ask.

"You tell me," Mamá says. "You looked kind of sad last night. Did something happen?"

"Yes," I say.

"Do you want to talk about it?"

"No," I say.

I open the cabinet where there's a shelf that's all tea. *Every lesbian needs a ridiculous amount of tea, and that goes double for a couple composed of two lesbians*, Mom always says. *It's in the manual they gave me when I came out. I can show you.*

Mamá rests her elbows on the counter. "Are you okay?"

"Yeah," I say, and my voice comes out as level as I feel. "I actually am."

Yes, my heart feels as raw as the landscape around the inlet. It's taken sun and wind, bleaching out like driftwood between storms.

But as much as Lore walking away left cracks in me, Lore's reaction wasn't the point. And I didn't know that until they walked away. The point was whether I could ever leave that much of me open to someone else. I told Lore how I feel about them for them, so they would know. But I told Lore how I feel about me for me. And even though the inside of me feels broken into little pieces of glitter, the jar of my heart still holds it all.

That's how I feel. Distinctly okay.

For about three hours.

In those few hours, I start pulling at the edges of what happened. I keep thinking about it. The weather in my brain shifts. It moves from the reassuring cloud cover of *I'm okay* to the glare of *I can't believe I did that.* I can't believe I showed Lore that much of me. I can't believe I brought them into the world under the lake again. I can't believe I thought revealing the chaos inside my own heart was a good idea.

I hate when my brain does this. I'm so sure I've let something go, I feel practically triumphant with having let it go. Then it comes rushing in as hard as I pushed it away. I forget things exist and then, with a shock of remembering, realize I can't forget they exist. They come out from behind the clouds and take up the whole sky.

I forget that I have a phone appointment with Dr. Robins until he calls me.

*Sound normal,* I tell myself.

"Heart rate feeling good?" he asks.

"Yeah," I say.

"Any irritability?" he asks.

"You mean more than usual?" I ask.

Dr. Robins laughs.

"No," I say.

"Good," he says. "Let me know if that changes. Are you still feeling good with your meds?"

"Yeah," I say.

He checks in on a few more details before asking, "Anything else we should talk about?"

I hesitate. But he lets the silence go long enough that I say, "Can I ask you something?"

"Sure," Dr. Robins says.

"What if what I've been doing for a long time stops working?" I ask.

"What do you mean?" Dr. Robins asks.

"I mean"—I pause to pin down how I want to ask this—"how do I know if what I'm doing is the right way to do things?"

Dr. Robins is quiet for a minute.

"Do you remember how you told me that testosterone felt like the right direction for you?" he asks.

"Yeah," I say.

"I think you're looking for the closest equivalent to that," he says. "Something that feels like the right direction, even if you don't completely know the path ahead. Does that make sense?"

I almost, on instinct, say *Yes*.

I almost fall into saying *Of course I understand.*

But I pause. I touch a piece of sea glass on my windowsill.

"No," I say.

"Okay," Dr. Robins says. No sigh. He just tries again. "If it has to do with your mental health care or your medical care, your meds or your hormones, anything like that, then please talk to me, talk to any of your doctors," he says. "But I think you might be talking about more than that."

"Yeah," I say, under my breath. I'm used to saying something when my meds feel off. It took a couple of tries to find the right one and the right dosage.

This is more about how I organize my own life in my own brain. How I put the pieces together or separate them out. How painted animals held in my hands are both evidence of an art form passed down from my great-grandfather, and the only place my bad days are allowed to exist.

"You talk to people you trust," Dr. Robins says.

"Whether that's us, or your parents, or someone else you know cares about your best interests."

It's such a Dr. Robins way to put it. *Someone else you know cares about your best interests.* But that's part of what I like about Dr. Robins. He's precise in how he puts things when he knows I need it, so my brain can't get lost in the ambiguity.

"You try things," Dr. Robins says. "And you figure out what works. And you accept that some things will work for a while and then stop working."

I think of how I have to constantly rearrange the index cards in my room so they don't become invisible to me.

"You try to remember that needing to change how you do things isn't a failure," Dr. Robins says. "Living with our own brains, it's work we do our whole lives. And an inherent part of that is accepting that some things just aren't going to work the same way forever. Some might. But some won't. Some things will work for someone else but not for you and the other way around. And figuring that out, that's part of adapting. You outgrow some things that helped you once. It doesn't necessarily make them bad, or wrong. It just means this is where you leave them. Or this is where they become something else."

I think of all the pieces it takes to help me work with my own brain. Therapy and classes. Medication that quiets my brain enough to let me do one thing, and then the next thing. Working with doctors. Pieces of paper tacked up on my walls. A different room for exams at school so I don't fixate on someone tapping a pen and so I don't annoy anyone with how I gesture or pace when I'm thinking. Wire and papier-mâché and paint. Important items left in my path so I don't walk out of my room without them.

Life with my brain is something I have to assemble. Like the index cards and clocks I move around my room, it never stays completely still.

When I'm off the phone, I feel a possibility hovering near me, like the electric potential between two charged points. I have a small window to change the weather in my brain.

I could make an alebrije.

But I don't.

Instead I call the brother who taught me to make them.

My sister-in-law picks up, and I tell her I want to come see Antonio.

"This is happening," Michelle says. "I'm feeding you. You're playing with the dogs. You're painting with Antonio. Now get your ass over here."

Like I usually do when I think of something important, I grab a piece of paper and write down a reminder. This is one I will stick directly to the backpack I'm bringing.

*Pack your injection supplies.*

It's an hour and a half on a bus between here and where

Antonio lives, so unless I want to make that trip back just for the vial and syringes, I need to pack everything.

Mamá sees me drawing little patterns on the edges of the note. She has the same smile as when she sees me pin up my index cards, like these small things are worth being proud of.

Mom and Mamá have known and loved things about me before I even understood them. Growing up, I found board games patience-thinningly slow, and when some adults told me I wasn't being friendly if I didn't play with everyone else, Mamá told me to go do something else, that it didn't matter if I liked what everyone else liked. When Mom taught me to drive, she didn't bang her forehead against the steering wheel horn. Even though I had an easier time understanding the mechanics of a combustion engine than learning how to start a car and pull onto the street.

When I forgot a binder or my boxer briefs in the washer and then ran downstairs before Mom or Mamá could find them, they pretended not to notice. They humored me during my desperate performances of sounding casual. *Sorry, I forgot I had a load in.*

But they knew. By the time I came out, their reaction was relief, not shock.

Once you get past the fear of being seen, you can get to the part where you know you're not alone.

# LORE

When the world under the lake doesn't show up again, I know it's a good thing.

But it still leaves a hollow in me, not finding Bastián in the middle of a street thick with seagrass. Or at the abandoned playground that's glowing at the edges. Or in the dark glittering with bubbles that float above us like lanterns.

So the next time Amanda the Learning Specialist asks if I want to talk about what happened at my last school, I don't have the clear space in me to craft a polite response. I forget to do the calibration, the screening of what I'm about to say. I answer before thinking about how a promising student worthy of a glowing report might respond.

"I'm not gonna cry in here," I say. "So if that's what I'm supposed to do, I don't know what to tell you."

"Why do you think I want you to cry in here?" Amanda the Learning Specialist asks.

"Why else would you ask me questions about it?" I say. "I'm sure you have a whole file on me. You already know what happened. And I'm not gonna try to defend it."

"What do you think you have to defend?" Amanda the Learning Specialist asks.

That catches me as off guard as a joke. "Really?"

Amanda the Learning Specialist looks sad in a way I want to pick apart, to root out any pity. But I can't find any. She just looks sad.

"The school should have protected you," she says. "You know that, right? The stuff that guy was doing to you, the stuff he was saying to you, not to mention that shit with your binder, that was harassment based on—"

"Stop." I hold up both my hands and shut my eyes.

If she keeps talking, I'll get pulled back into what happened. There will be none of me left in this room. There isn't even enough of me here now to appreciate Amanda the Learning Specialist saying the word *shit*.

Amanda the Learning Specialist leaves the silence for a minute, like she's waiting for me to talk.

I don't.

So she does.

"You know, there's a quote from one of my favorite poets," she says. "Whatever is unnamed, this will become, not merely unspoken, but unspeakable."

"I did speak it," I say. "I told who I was supposed to tell." My shoulders round. I want to disappear into the shell of my own body. "They said it was just talk, that if I didn't react, or reacted the right way, they'd lose interest. They said the same thing to my parents."

I study the faded pattern on the carpet. "You want to know how well that worked? After what happened? They started following me. And every time I looked over my shoulder . . ." The thread of their laughter is still so loud in my brain it makes me close my eyes. "They said the only reason they didn't beat me up to get back at me for what I did to their friend was . . ." I shut my eyes again. I can't say it. I try again. "They said I was lucky I was . . ."

I still can't say it.

After a few seconds that feel like a full minute, Amanda the Learning Specialist says, "You fighting back doesn't justify anyone trying to make you afraid."

I shake my head to clear the memory, the prickling through my shoulder blades when I could feel them behind me, knowing that me looking over my shoulder to check was exactly what they wanted.

Maybe this will always be the space I live in, wanting to look back, knowing I never can.

# BASTIÁN

"**A**ct now." Michelle comes into the living room with a stack of sheets. "If you put these down for a minute, the dogs will sit on them."

"And by the dogs you mean Clover," I say.

"Accurate." Michelle hands me the sheets and goes back into the kitchen.

Lucky, the sheepdog mix Antonio's had for years, sleeps half the day and ambles around the house or yard the other. Clover's the tiny one who still gets into things, including backpacks. Because of everything I brought for my shot, I'll be triple-checking that I close mine.

I've gotten the bottom sheet on the sofa when I notice Antonio watching me.

My brother has an unnerving way of inventorying my features, seeing what they add up to.

I tuck the end of the top sheet under the sofa cush-
ions. "Yes?"

"Nothing," he says. "There's just something different
about you."

"Yeah," I say, thinking of the list of supplies I triple-
checked. Vial. Syringes. Needles. Alcohol prep pads. Band-
Aids. And I probably still forgot something. "I told you."

"No," Antonio says. "It's not just that."

I pull on the pillowcases.

"I think you're ready," Antonio says.

"For what?" I ask.

He gestures for me to follow him, which I do, into
the room where he and Michelle keep their yet-to-be-
unpacked boxes.

Antonio starts looking through one, but I'm not watching him.

I'm too busy taking in all the points of color in this
room.

An iguana with a tail that ends in the perfect bulb
of a paper flame. A rabbit with a quetzal's tail feathers.
A porcupine with every quill a different shade. A cross
between a rattlesnake and a butterfly. There must be a
hundred alebrijes on the windowsills, on an old dresser,
clustered on top of boxes.

"You kept the alebrijes?" I ask.

He laughs. "Not all of them," he says. "If I kept them

all I wouldn't have room for anything else. I've given a lot of them to relatives. A few of our cousins really like them. Those are just the ones I made for me." He closes a box and opens another one. "Mostly the ones I made on bad days."

"Yeah, but you kept them? Why?" I ask. I'm stumbling over the words because I don't want to ask what I'm thinking.

*You kept your bad days?*

Antonio sifts through another box. "What else would I do with them?"

"But you never had them out at your apartment," I say.

"There was no place to put anything at that apartment," he says. "I would've kept knocking them over."

"But you told me you made them when you were mad about things, or frustrated, or just sad, right?" I ask. "Wasn't the whole point to get rid of all that?"

"Not to get rid of it." He folds down the flaps on a box. "But to feel like it wasn't taking up all the space in me, yeah."

"Then why did you keep them?" I ask.

Antonio looks at me like I've asked something both obvious and not easily answerable. *Why do we breathe air instead of water? Why can't I get to Saturn on the same bus I took here? What elevation do unicorns typically live at?*

"Because they're still part of me, Bastián," he says.

"My bad days, they're part of me. And the things I make, those are part of me too. Especially the things I made during bad days, because they remind me that I still made something out of those bad days."

For a minute, my brain is quiet. There's nothing but the colors of the alebrijes, and the sound of cardboard whisking against cardboard, and my brother's words.

*I still made something out of those bad days.*

I spend so much of my life fighting my bad days. I thought they had to be as distinct from me as land from water.

But I can't keep separating out my hardest days like they're a shadow version of me. Days where my brain finds its way forward, and days where it gets stuck in a feeling I can't pull back from, these are part of the cycles that come with my ADHD. And even though right now I know this down to my cells, there will be days when I don't know it. Today, I may accept how my brain works. Tomorrow, I may be fighting it again. There will be days when I feel proud and worthy, and days I feel frustrated and defeated and lost.

The chaos in my brain doesn't turn like a moon cycle. The determination and the discouragement don't come in and out with the tidal rhythm of an ocean. They move with the seeming randomness of lake seiches.

But I can love who I love. I can do what makes the inside of me glow like sea glass. I can keep talking to the people who care about me. I can do the work that helps me live with the seiches inside my own brain.

These are the points of light I follow. They leave space for the possibility that all my days are worth keeping.

"Found it." From another open box, Antonio pulls a fold of dark denim.

The jean jacket I remember him wearing for years. He's wearing it in half the pictures of us when I was growing up. The stiff edges of the collar and cuffs have softened from how many times it's gone through the wash.

"Take it," he says.

"What?" I ask.

"It's yours now," Antonio says.

I didn't think I could be struck even more silent than I was a minute ago.

This jacket, the easy way Antonio shrugged into it and out of it, the way his cologne got woven into the threads, this jacket holds so much of what makes my brother my brother. How he was known for being a blur of speed on the football field, and for bringing bunches of our over-grown rosemary to neighbors just because he felt like it. That's the kind of masculinity I wanted, my equivalent of my brother in that jacket.

"Come on, take it." Antonio laughs, shoving it into my hand. "I think it's gonna look good on you."

The fabric is thick and heavy but soft in my hands.

It's one more thread between him and me, just like

the alebrijes are a thread between our great-grandfather and us. Maybe our bisabuelo did the same thing we do, generations before we were born. Maybe he took what was spilling out of his heart and made it into fins and wings. And I think it might be this that I've seen in my brother for so long. It's the glowing center of Antonio, the alchemy not just of giving shape and color to his hardest moments, but of being a man who leaves space for his own heart.

I put on Antonio's jacket, and I feel a little closer to being not just more like my brother, but more like the version of myself I'm meant to be.

# LORE

ore."

I turn at the sound of my name outside the hardware store.

Vivienne waves. She's holding paper coffee cups like she's waiting for someone, but still crosses the sidewalk toward me.

"Where have you vanished to?" she asks.

"Just helping my parents with some stuff." I lift the bag I took out of the hardware store. "It's been busy."

Vivienne glances down the sidewalk, then back at me. "Can I ask you something?"

"Yeah," I say.

Vivienne steps close enough that I can see the texture of her sweater, the weave of the lavender cloth. "What happened?" she asks. "What did they do?"

"What do you mean?" I ask.

"Bastián," Vivienne says. "What did they do that was worth just disappearing on them?"

"Nothing," I say. "Bastián didn't do anything. I just don't like them like that."

"I'm not talking about that," Vivienne says. "If you're not into the boy, you're not. That's fine. But why just drop all of us? We kind of like you, in case you didn't notice."

I look down at our shoes, and I think they're the exact same kind, except mine are my favorite shade of brown, and Vivienne's are strawberry-milkshake pink.

"It's a long story," I say.

A long story that starts with Bastián being Abril and Vivienne and Sloan and Maddie's friend first. If I can't be around Bastián, I can't be friends with them.

I glance around, hoping that whoever Vivienne is waiting for is Abril. Or Sloan. Or Maddie.

Vivienne must pick up on that. "If you're worried about seeing them," she says, "you don't need to be. Bastián's at their brother's house."

"Oh," I say. "Okay."

"Look." Vivienne sets down both coffee cups on an old newspaper box that holds the local weekly. "If you change your mind about being friends, I'm around." She rips the cardboard sleeve off one cup and scrawls things on it, not just her number but her address, like we're the kind of friends who might just stop by to see each other.

I do not return the favor. I can see it now, my incomprehensible scrawl alongside Vivienne's bubbly handwriting.

When I get home, my workbook from Amanda the Learning Specialist is glowering from a corner of the kitchen. Another reminder of my terrible handwriting.

I shove it in with the cookbooks.

I wash the dishes in the sink. I dry my mom's favorite cup, blue with painted orange flowers. These small things—the familiar rhythm of dishes, slicing limón into water, hanging the clock in our kitchen—these things keep me steady. They're helping me narrow my world to what's in front of me—pieces in the workroom, pages of summer reading, the grocery list.

The cups click against one another as I put them away. I close the cabinet door, leaving nothing between me and my view of the fridge.

I didn't realize until now how easy it would be to get up there.

I jump up on the counter.

I climb on top of the fridge.

When my dad comes into the kitchen, it takes him a second to register me.

"Should I be concerned?" he asks.

I settle into sitting, making sure my feet don't knock the magnets off the front. "Someone told me it helps you see things differently."

"Is it working?" my dad asks.

From here, the books that seem big enough to block out the sun are as small as stamps on an envelope. From here, everything we had to move could be toy furniture, instead of all the weight we had to haul from the last version of our lives to this one.

The appointment marked on the wall calendar for tomorrow isn't a square of pure dread.

It's just a place I have to show up.

"I think so." I look down. The squares of vinyl flooring look as small as my hands.

And the workbook Amanda the Learning Specialist gave me looks small enough for me to hold.

"Will you hand me that?" I ask, pointing to the thin spine sticking out from the cookbooks.

My dad passes it to me.

"Thanks." I pull out the pen I tucked into the spiral binding. I cross my legs into me. I open to the first page.

# BASTIÁN

*I am the orange.*

When I think this, I'm back in my parents' kitchen, practicing. Not sitting on the edge of the bathtub in my brother's house.

I run an alcohol pad over my leg, the chill instant on my skin. I swipe one over the top of the vial. I prep everything just like I did with Lore.

I dart the needle in. I do the injection. It's a breath going through my body, the deep, glowing blue of something being right.

I walk around Antonio's neighborhood, because that's what I do when there's too much of any feeling in me. Even good ones, like the relief that I just did that, can feel so big I have to move around to clear some of it.

When I come back, Antonio's ripping pages out of a phone book and covering the kitchen table. "You ready?"

Something in me feels still, and settled.

"Yeah," I say. "I am."

We shape the wire frames, mold the papier-mâché, mix the paint. I'm wearing my brother's jacket, sleeves cuffed so they don't pick up a film of papier-mâché or streaks of paint while we do the work of our great-grandfather's hands.

Antonio holds up two figures that are shaped a lot like Clover and Lucky. "What do you think?"

"Museumworthy," I say. "Your dogs will go down in history as famous muses."

"Thought so," Antonio says.

My fingers are steady as I paint the first alebrije, an armadillo the color of lilac blossoms, with blue dragonfly wings and eyes like embers.

For once, I'm not imagining setting this one down on the sea glass path, watching it carry away a piece of myself I think I don't need. I let the alebrijes be wonders all on their own. A hummingbird with fins. An axolotl with a tongue like a flame.

"Hey, Antonio?" I say.

"Yeah?" Antonio says, not looking up.

"Thank you," I say.

He looks up. "For what?"

This is one of those times where I said something

without thinking, which means I don't quite know how to explain it. So I slow down, and I try to figure it out.

Antonio knows these pauses, so he goes back to his alebrije. He knows I never figure out what I need to figure out while someone's staring at me.

Things in my brain are always colliding. It makes it harder to put information in any kind of order. But this, making alebrijes, is where I get to welcome those collisions instead of resisting them. My brain gets to imagine unexpected combinations, a fox with a peacock's tail, or a doe with a narwhal's horn.

Antonio gave those collisions something to do.

"For this," I say. "I don't know if I ever said thank you for all this."

I work at giving more detail on the wings, darker blue veining out within the lighter blue.

I don't realize I've gotten up until Antonio laughs.

I stop, registering that I'm walking back and forth while painting. "Sorry."

"Don't be." Antonio shapes a fish's fin. "I like that you don't sit still."

"You do?" I ask.

"Yeah." He works on the edge of the fin. "It's like you're always ready for what's next."

Usually, my binder feels like the thing holding me together, keeping me in when my brain throws me in so many directions I feel like I'm flying apart.

But right now, in my brother's jacket, this is a little like the first time I put a binder on. Not just the wonder of how, beneath a T-shirt, my body could have belonged to so many other guys. But remembering that I *was* a guy. I was who I knew I was.

In this kitchen, I'm like my brother. I'm like my great-grandfather. I'm one of the Silvano men, dreaming with paint on our hands.

# LORE

I throw my bag on the low table in Amanda the Learning Specialist's office. "Here." I hand her the workbook. "Warning, I don't have cute handwriting. I don't dot my *i*'s with hearts or little circles. My dad says I have the handwriting of a doctor scribbling on a chart with their nondominant hand, and I'm pretty sure he's being nice."

Amanda the Learning Specialist takes the workbook. "You know it's really common for people with dyslexia to have messy handwriting, right?"

"Not like that," I say.

"Yes, like that." She turns through the workbook. "Sometimes exactly like that."

I pull out a picture book with worn purple edges.

I hand it to her.

"You wanted me to bring my favorite book, and this is my favorite book," I say, and it feels like confessing to something. "I was nine when I first read it."

I could read it all the way through. No stops. No catching. Phonics had dismantled the way I had learned to read, cracking it into so many pieces I thought I was too stupid for books. But I could still read this book.

"And a lot of those are sight words." I don't mean to sound as defensive as I do, but I can't help it. "So no one could tell me I was reading them wrong."

It's not just the dyslexia that makes reading harder. It's how the world responds to it. I learned how to read, but then got told I was reading wrong, that I had to read another way no matter how hard my brain fought it. So even now, when I read, I bring with me not just my dyslexia, but also my fear that I am reading wrong. I bring with me the flinch of hiding picture books in my backpack, knowing what other kids my age would say.

Amanda the Learning Specialist reviews the pages about a rabbit diving into different tubs of paint, turning herself sea blue and then flower purple. Turning herself leaf green. But the color she likes best, the one that happens when she mixes all the paints, is brown. To her, it's warm, and perfect. Not dirty. Not wrong. To her, the color brown is beautiful.

I almost miss it, the unclenching in the center of my heart. That easing up doesn't come from Amanda the

Learning Specialist saying that this being my favorite book is okay. And she does. She tells me how anyone who made fun of me reading picture books didn't know what they were talking about, how she wishes everyone read them.

But what Amanda the Learning Specialist says, that's not the point. The point is me showing this book to her in the first place. It's the strange physics of all this, how something in me releases not because of her reaction, but my action.

On the bus home, the rain against the windows is a drizzle so light it could be the spray thrown by passing cars. When we stop, and the bus door whooshes open, I smell pine needles. As a few people get on—two old ladies, a guy who looks like he's in his twenties—I can see the deep green needles coated in tiny points of rain.

The old ladies' mix of perfumes—the same kind of flowery as my mom's favorite detergent—goes by. The guy in his twenties takes a seat behind me.

As the bus gets up to speed, the guy makes a noise toward me, one meant to tell me he likes what he sees.

There's not really any way I ever look that lets me move through the world without resistance. Sometimes I look like a boy who's even younger than I actually am, a boy with soft edges and floppy hair and a shrug in my posture that makes people think they can shove me aside.

Or I look like a girl who men think they have a right to stare at.

I know which one I look like today. Black sweater over a tank top with scalloped lace around the edges. My favorite sheer red lip gloss. Tighter jeans than I wear when I'm feeling more like a guy. Hair down, and that I'm already regretting I didn't pull into a ponytail before I left Amanda the Learning Specialist's office, but then again, that would leave the heat of his gaze on my bare neck.

"Not feeling friendly?" the guys asks.

The humming from the floor of the bus rises into my body.

"Come on," he says. "Just give me a smile."

When I shut my eyes, the hum of the bus turns to a breaking sound, like wood splintering apart.

The sound of Merritt and his friends laughing radiates out from the seats and windows.

If it had just been them laughing, I could have withstood it. I knew how to take the laughing, absorb it. I'd been taking it since third grade.

It was the threat held in all that noise, the promise that if they ever got bored with laughing at me, with following me, they'd do worse.

"Just turn around," the guy behind me says.

I squeeze my eyes shut tighter.

The first time I threw my fist into Merritt Harnish, he and the guys who followed him around forgave it, or forgave it enough. We were kids, all gawky limbs and entropy, so they eventually let it go, content with how they could make my shoulders round with a few words.

But the second time, that they couldn't forgive. That was serious. That was real. We were too old for them to pretend it wasn't. And instead of being in front of a girl Merritt liked, it was in front of half the school.

Now this guy behind me, trying to get me to turn around, is all of them. He wants what I didn't give them last year, and if I give it to him, I'll give it to all of them.

"Turn around and look at me, beautiful," he says, his voice holding all of theirs.

He wants me to look back.

He wants to see the fear in me.

My brain feels carved out of salt-soaked wood, brittle and splintering into even smaller pieces.

Then one of those pieces breaks against another, and I remember.

When I stared at Merritt, he froze. I made him see me—as a boy, as someone whose stare held a hundred shades of brown—and he froze.

This whole time, I've thought that I hated myself for fighting back. But I think I've hated myself more for what that fighting back meant. It was the end of a story other people wrote, and I gave it to them, that perfect ending.

When Merritt and his friends started with me, I asked for help. And I got told to laugh off the taunts, to learn to laugh at myself along with those guys. So I did. I laughed. Until I couldn't anymore. And when I fought back, when everyone saw me hit Merritt first, I confirmed everything that so many people watching already thought. With that first hit, I became everything they expected of someone brown and trans and dyslexic. They wielded everything about me against me until I did something definitive enough to prove I was the problem all along.

In that moment, I participated in the process of making myself that problem, the same way I participated when I laughed with Merritt and his friends. I became part of a story that placed me exactly where everyone else wanted me.

I grip the edge of the seat.

I look over my shoulder, at the guy who's been talking to my hair and the back of my sweater.

He grins. "Was that so hard?"

I stare, eyes wide and boring into him.

"Now how about a smile?" he asks.

I don't smile.

"What?" he asks.

My eyes augur into him. He's a layer of ice in my way.

He gives a thin, nervous laugh. "Okay, you can turn back around now."

Like I was waiting for permission.

I don't laugh with him.

I give him nothing.

My own laugh has been haunting me, but there's been so much under that laugh. That laugh has been the ghost reminding me how much I stopped being on my own side. I learned that I couldn't trust myself with myself. I became one of those laughing voices, one of my own bullies.

I have been haunted by that version of myself. But I can't exile them forever, no more than Bastián can exile themself from every time their ADHD was a current pulling them under. So many of us are haunted by versions of ourselves we wish we could exile. But the pieces of our beings don't pull apart that easily. If we try to unweave ourselves, we unravel at the edges. So we all do the work of reconciling who we are now with the ghosts we once were.

One day, I can earn back my own trust.

I can start now.

I keep staring.

"What are you staring at me like that for?" the guy asks.

I make him nervous, but he can't not look at me. I make him look at me. I stay turned around. I keep looking back.

"What's wrong with you?" he asks.

He wanted to see me, so I make him see me.

"Stop doing that," he says.

I keep staring at him, my fingers gripping the back of the seat.

This whole time, I thought if I looked back, Merritt and his friends would win.

But when I look back, really look, guys who think they're fearless recoil.

I keep staring.

When this guy looks at me, he sees a brown girl. And I am a brown girl, just like I'm a brown boy, just like I'm both and neither, in different proportions depending on the day. I'm the gradients of blue and green and violet and silver that the lake turns.

But he doesn't know that, because he doesn't know me. He sees the hair, the lip gloss, the eyeliner, the lace on the edge of my tank top, and he sees a brown girl who he should get to look at. He sees a brown girl staring at him as shamelessly as he was just staring at me, except my stare has none of the admiration. This surprises and confuses and scares him so much that he will not realize how insulted he feels until hours later, when I am long gone and he has blurred me together so completely with other brown girls that he cannot tell us apart.

I keep staring. And he keeps moving his eyes around, looking ahead, or out the window, or the window on the opposite side, or trying to catch the eye of another passenger. He tries to get a sympathetic look from any of them, a shared, unspoken *Can you believe this bitch?*

But none of them are having it. Two friends, in the middle of figuring out when they're getting coffee together, sneer at him like he's interrupting. A parent, encouraging a child who works at a bead maze, pauses only to glare at him. An older passenger sticks to his newspaper, pointedly turning the page. I can't be sure from this angle, but I think when the guy tries with the driver, the driver only casts a cold glance in the convex mirror. Even las viejas who got on at the same stop give him twin admonishing expressions.

They all saw him, and heard him.

I know what I've just done, so I settle into my seat. I know I can't get off this bus until after he has. I can't get off, even at my stop, and risk him following me. Even if I'm as reckless right now as my stare is unyielding, the instinct in my chest warns me that I have to stay with the people on this bus rather than risk him following me.

So I keep staring. I might as well keep staring.

But as the bus slows into the next stop, he scrambles to his feet. He lurches toward the door. He stumbles off like he's running away.

I watch him watch the bus pull away, fear and confusion in his face.

I turn and sit straight. I look forward.

If I leave everything that happened behind me, if I draw hard lines between *there* and *here*, *then* and *now*, I leave behind that moment where I made Merritt look at me. I lose that moment when the force of me was so unfathomable he couldn't do anything except stay still and watch. If I forget everything that happened before my family moved, I'll lose that brazen thread inside me, bright as a wire filament.

At the next transfer point, the bus sits for a minute, the driver holding to keep the schedule.

I look out the window. The trees grow so far into the road they're brushing the side of the bus. It's stopped raining, but perfectly round drops glitter at the very ends of the pine needles, shining wet.

A flash of color darts in and out of the branches. When it settles long enough, I get a better look. A tiny butterfly, the outer wings silvery brown like the lake's shoreline, the inner wings blue as the leaves of water that lifted off the surface. Each time the butterfly lands or takes off, the slight weight knocks loose a drop of rain.

A week ago, those points of rain would have looked like beads of clear glass.

But right now, those raindrops at the ends of the pine needles look so much like the little bubbles Bastián and I eased out of the syringes that I almost laugh.

I get off the bus, five stops early. I tell the driver "Thank you" on my way out, like this was my planned destination the whole time.

*Once you know the right thing, every minute you don't do it feels wrong.*

I make two calls.

My first is to Vivienne.

"You know the thing you thought I was gonna do the first time I asked you and Abril where to find Bastián?" I ask when she picks up.

"The grand romantic gesture?" she asks.

"Yeah," I say. "I mean, kind of. I don't know about the romantic part. I don't know how Bastián feels anymore. And I don't care. I mean, I do care, but even if they don't feel that way, I want to be friends if they want to be friends. I made a mistake, and I want to fix it, and I'm afraid if I don't do it now I'll lose my nerve to ever do it. So just be blunt here, is this a good idea or bad idea?"

The silence makes me suspect that I said too much at once. A few seconds more, and I'm sure of it.

"Vivienne?" I ask.

Voices chatter in the background.

"Is someone else there with you?" I ask.

"Yeah," Vivienne says. "We're all over at my house. We would have invited you if you weren't avoiding all of us." I can hear the smug smile in her voice. "Can I tell them?" Just like that, the smug smile is gone from her voice.

It takes me a second to register what she means. "Tell them—what I just told you?"

"Yeah," Vivienne says. "Up to you. I can either give you my opinion or we can get a group vote."

I hesitate. But Bastián's four closest friends might know better than one of them.

"Fine," I say. "Go ahead."

Voices murmur in the background. I can barely hear them over the traffic.

"The consensus says do it," Vivienne says.

"Okay," I say. "So what do I do?"

"Where are you?" Vivienne asks.

I give her the stop number, the rough location.

Vivienne repeats what I just said to everyone else.

"Maddie knows where you are," Vivienne says. "And she says you're gonna want to write this down."

"Write what down?" I ask.

"How to get to Antonio and Michelle's," Vivienne says.

"You want me to show up unannounced at their brother's house?" I ask.

"Yeah," Vivienne says. "Show them you're showing up. Literally, in this case."

I don't realize until she says it how much I was both hoping and dreading that she'd suggest this. It's a simultaneous rise and fall, two vertical drafts blowing past each other inside a storm.

"No," I say. "Forget it. Never mind."

"Lore," she says.

"We've crossed into bad idea," I say. "I don't know their brother. I'm not just gonna stop by without permission."

"Good point," Vivienne says.

I breathe out. "Thank you."

I'm already calculating how long it'll probably be until I can get the next bus home.

Except that Vivienne is still talking to everyone else, and hasn't hung up.

"What are you all doing?" I ask.

"Hold on," Vivienne says. "Sloan's calling Bastián's brother."

"What?" I ask, loud enough that a woman on a nearby bench looks up from her book. I lower my voice again. "Why?"

"You don't want to show up without permission," Vivienne says. "I respect that. So we're asking permission."

"Seriously?" I ask.

"Yeah, Sloan and Maddie's older brother know Antonio pretty well, so they kind of do too," Vivienne says.

"Then *they* can show up unannounced," I say.

More voices in the background.

"Vivienne?" At this point I'm whisper-yelling.

After a few more seconds, Vivienne says, "Yeah, five votes for this being a good idea."

"Five?" I ask.

"Yeah," Vivienne says. "Me, Abril, Maddie, and Sloan just called Antonio, and Antonio says come over."

"Wait, why doesn't Bastián get a vote?" I ask.

"Antonio didn't ask them," Vivienne says.

"Why not?" I ask.

"Oh, Lore," Vivienne says with fond patience. "I haven't known you very long, but I think I know that if Bastián knows you're coming, you're definitely gonna lose your nerve." This time, a sympathetic sigh. "I think you know I'm right about this."

I kick at the dirt near my feet. "What if Bastián doesn't want me there?"

"Then you get on the next bus back," she says, "and you come over here, because no matter what happens with you and Bastián we're still their friends and we're still yours, okay? All of that clear? Now get a pen."

I grab a pen from my bag. The next thing my hand finds is the cardboard sleeve Vivienne wrote her address on. I let out a laugh.

"What?" Vivienne asks.

"Nothing," I say. "Go ahead."

Vivienne puts Maddie on the phone, and Maddie gives me the bus number, the approximate next time, the stop to get off at.

My heart feels fragile as a soap bubble. "You're sure about this?" I ask.

"We're hanging up on you now," Maddie says. "Go."

My second call is to my parents.

"So, what if I wasn't home until later?" I ask.

"How much later?" my mom asks.

I do a quick calculation of the bus transfer times. "A lot."

"Why?" my mom asks.

"Because I'm thinking about doing something stupid," I say.

"The good kind of stupid or the bad kind?" she asks.

"The go-tell-my-friend-I-care-about-them-because-I-don't-think-they-know kind."

"That's the good kind," my mother says. And then she says the same word Maddie hung up with. "Go."

# BASTIÁN

As soon as the doorbell rings, Clover starts barking.

"Can you get that?" Antonio asks.

I hold up my hands, blotched in blue from the gradient of the dragonfly wings, and bright green from what I'm working on now. "Really?"

Clover's sharp, small bark gets louder.

Antonio holds up his own hands, covered with purple and burgundy.

"Yeah, that's worse," I say. I wipe my fingers off, but not much comes away.

I don't realize until I'm almost to the door that the alebrije I'm working on is still in my left hand, like a cup I thought I'd put down.

I open the door anyway.

"Hi," Lore says.

The air from outside is laced with the sawdust-and-green-apple smell I've come to think of as Lore. It weaves together with the smell of the camellia bushes.

"Hi," I say.

"So what's your gender today?" Lore asks, like it's *How are you?*

"You came all this way to ask me my gender forecast?"

Lore doesn't flinch. "Well?"

I shrug. "Nonbinary with a chance of stars?"

Lore smiles.

"You?" I ask.

"I don't know," Lore says. "I'll tell you when I figure it out."

"Do you want to come in?" I ask.

"I don't know," Lore says. "I'll tell you when I figure it out."

I laugh.

They laugh.

The way Lore looks at me sends a charge through me. The memory of them kissing me flares hot on my tongue. My brain calls up the feeling of their palms on my shoulder blades, my hands on their waist, just below their rib cage.

Clover trots around our legs, barking at Lore.

Lore looks down, wary.

"She sounds like she hates everyone, but she doesn't," I say.

Lore looks back up at me, but their eyes pause on what I'm holding.

I have the sudden impulse to hide the alebrije in my palm.

The glow-in-the-dark green cat matches the ones in the art photo Lore showed me.

I meant what I told them in the world under the lake. I didn't care if Lore didn't want me kissing them anymore. I just wanted to be in Lore's life. I wanted to be close enough to feel the pull of them like a current.

Except now I'm almost positive that this tiny cat is about to scare them off. Lore now knows how deep they got into me. They know that green cats and orange fish and red foxes are part of the landscape of my dreams.

The way Lore stares at my fingers, and the tiny version of one of the radioactive cats, makes me pretty sure that no matter why they came here, they're about to bolt.

I am already bracing for how much this will hurt, worse than Lore walking away from the world under the lake. I brought Lore there, but they came here, and might now be in the process of changing their mind about whatever made them decide to.

But the intent way they're looking, it's like they're studying something, not recoiling from it. Lore's not shifting their weight like they're pulling back. They're coming closer, like they're putting something together.

# LORE

On top of a bookshelf I can see from the door, alebrijes dry on what looks like old newspaper. No. Phone book pages. There are coyotes with wings and jaguars with narwhal horns that look a lot like ones Bastián has made. But they're painted and patterned in a slightly different style.

The ones that look like Bastián's work are alongside them. Red and gray foxes. Orange and turquoise goldfish with fins of sculpted paper. More bright green cats that match the one Bastián is holding.

The pictures I showed Bastián. They stuck with them enough that they made these versions of them.

The nervous way Bastián turns the green cat in their hands, the rustling newspaper underneath the fish and foxes, all of it put together breaks me open like a glitter jar. The dyed water, all the sparkly pieces, the glue, all of it spills out of me and goes everywhere.

"I lied, okay?" I say.

"What?" Bastián asks. I don't know if they want clarification or didn't hear me over the small dog barking at me.

"I do feel that way about you," I say. "I do like you like that. And I like you as a friend too, and I want to be whatever we end up being, because I like you every way I've gotten to know you—" I stop midsentence. I look down at the dog barking at me, louder now. She would be cute, halfway between a fox and a small bear, if she didn't sound like she wanted to bite my hand off. I have backed away from the door and into the front yard, but this seems to have angered her more.

I shrug at the dog. "What am I doing wrong here?"

"You're not doing anything wrong," Bastián says. "She wants you to pick her up."

I look back down at the dog, her barking quaking her whole body. "Really?"

"Yeah," Bastián says. "I know it doesn't sound like it. And you don't have to, by the way, I just wanted you to know."

I crouch down and carefully pick up the bear-fox-dog, her reddish fur even brighter against my sweater. I tense, still wondering if she'll bite me. But she's instantly quiet.

"So what I didn't want you to know," I say, getting used to the dog's weight in my arms, "it starts about third, fourth grade. Teachers started noticing that I wasn't"—I try to figure out how to phrase this—"they called it *decoding* words. Instead, I was saying back words I had memorized by sight. And when I was supposed to decode . . ."

I don't finish the sentence. Bastián heard the taunts. The world under the lake floated them to the surface.

I shift my weight, moving my body back and forth like I would to calm a baby. The dog is still quiet.

Bastián puts the green cat on the edge of a retaining wall, the painted feet in the grass sprouting between bricks. I can tell they're doing it to show that they're listening, but I want to tell them that I know they're still listening when they're fidgeting. Sometimes Bastián turning something over in their hands is a sign that they're listening.

Bastián looks at me, and what I need to say next makes the distance between them and me seem as wide as the space between galaxies.

I let the heat and dust held tight inside my heart break open into a whole universe. I tell Bastián. It's rambling and messy, but I say it. Merritt. Jilly Uhlenbruck's laugh. What I was running from the day Bastián and I met, how that was the first time I ended up with someone else's blood dotting my knuckles. How the last time I ended up with someone else's blood on my knuckles, it was my fist against Merritt's face, and then threats from all his friends.

The wind combs its fingers through Bastián's hair,

fluffing pieces off their forehead. Bastián doesn't ask questions. They just listen.

"That's what happened," I say. "That's what I didn't want you to know, because I thought there was no going forward if I ever looked back. And you knowing, that felt like looking back."

Bastián puts their hands in their pockets.

I shift my weight again, the dog watching me, and then watching Bastián.

"Please say something," I say.

Bastián shakes their head at the ground between our feet. They look almost impressed.

"What?" I ask.

"You kicked his ass," Bastián says in wonder.

Their laugh is small and slight, but it pulls me in, so I'm almost laughing too by the time I ask, "That's what you're taking away from this story?"

"A little bit," Bastián says. "Yeah."

"It's not something I'm supposed to be proud of," I say.

"I'm not laughing because it's funny," Bastián says. "I'm laughing because you did something so many of us have wanted to do."

"What do you mean?" I ask.

"He was a bully, and you fought back," Bastián says. "Do you know how many of us have wanted to do that?"

I don't ask what they mean by *us*. Those of us who are brown, trans, nonbinary, queer. Those of us who have brains that work in ways we want to explain but sometimes can't. Any of it. All of it.

"It's not like it went well," I say. "After that, everything unraveled."

"I know that." Bastián's not laughing now, not even a little. "You fought back because no one else was fighting for you. That part of you that wouldn't take it, that part was trying to protect you. So if you want to know what I take away from that story, it's that you made someone afraid of you who wanted to make you afraid."

The dog I'm still holding is watching Bastián, just like I am.

"You said that every way you've gotten to know me, you like me," Bastián says. "Same here. Every way. Including this one."

"But I did something stupid," I say. "I stopped thinking. That's the difference between you and me. You think, and sometimes I just stop thinking."

Now Bastián's laugh is louder, fuller. When the dog alerts, I think it's because of Bastián's laugh. But then I hear what I'm guessing is Bastián's sister-in-law calling, "Clover."

I put Clover down, and she scampers around the side of the house.

"What's funny?" I ask Bastián.

"Do you know what I have to do to make my brain work?" Bastián says. "I have timers telling me when to pack up my bag for work or for school. I have notes on light switches reminding me to eat and drink water. You saw them. I do my laundry on the same day every week because otherwise I just forget. Sometimes I have to literally bite my tongue so I don't interrupt people. I show up half an hour early to everything because if I don't, I'm two hours late, because sometimes my brain can't tell the difference between one hour and four."

Bastián sits on the edge of the retaining wall in the yard. The wind makes the shadows of a camellia bush shift over them.

"I paint alebrijes when I am out of patience with everything, including myself," Bastián says. "I use glitter jars to calm myself down the same way I did when I was little. I still have trouble sitting still. I have to plan how to get somewhere three times because directions make no sense to me. That's why I needed your help with the instructions for my shot, because my brain couldn't put the pieces together."

Bastián looks down at their pants, green paint on the belt loops and near where they slid their hands into their pockets. "Or that." Bastián spreads their hands, green coating their fingers. "See? I'll just forget things."

I sit next to Bastián, bracing my palms on the edge of the retaining wall. "Do you want to be touched right now?" I ask.

Bastián nods. "Do you?"

I nod back, and I try to brush a streak of wet paint off Bastián's face.

Bastián reaches a hand toward my face, then pulls it back. They look at the paint on their palm and fingers. "Sorry. I keep forgetting."

I pull their hand back toward me, slipping their palm onto my cheek and their fingers into my hair. Their skin is warm against mine and the paint is cool, and the inside of me is glitter spinning against dark water.

# BASTIÁN

**W**hen Lore kisses me, and I kiss Lore back, we hold a whole sky of light between us. It's bright as the surface of the lake and deep blue as the world underneath it.

When we stop, it's because we're laughing. I don't know exactly why we're laughing, but we are. Maybe it's because my fingers just got paint on Lore's cheek, and in their hair. Lore sets their forehead against mine, a comet of green crossing their eyebrow.

Or maybe it's Lore feeling what I'm feeling, something unfamiliar but that I'm meeting with recognition.

There's a certain way that falling for someone can only ever feel when you've fallen at least a little for yourself first. So maybe it's that flickering inside me, and inside

Lore too, how we had to know something for ourselves before knowing it with someone else.

The camellia bushes cast patterns on our arms, and the way Lore touches me is so soft and careful that when I shut my eyes, I can't tell the different between the changes in sun and shadow, and their hands.

# LORE

n every bus ride back from the learning specialist, I put in headphones. I listen to the summer reading the way my mother reads, a paper
copy of the book on my lap, following along as I listen.
Reading in two ways at once.

I track the lines from one page to the next. I hear the
words at the same time that my eyes take them in. I read
like my brain wants to read, in whole words and phrases.
And I might be imagining it, but the pages seem to have
a tint of blue and purple light at the corners, like when
I opened the book and found a little piece of the world
under the lake.

Just before my stop, I pause the audiobook. I mark my
place in the paper book.

I get off the bus and go down to the lake.

Before Bastián gets back from Antonio's, there's something I have to do.

I've gotten to love this corner of the lake. The brush on the hills turns gold in the afternoon and silver at night. The wind fluffs the hair sticking out of my hat. Purple and yellow balls of verbena dot the hills, and the bell-shaped flowers of desert willow spring up between rocks.

I brush the dust off the LAKELORE sign. I clear as much of the dirt as I can.

The sun finds the glitter jar in my bag, turning the sequins to copper coins as I open a tiny can of paint.

My mom and dad and I debated different options. The violet red of a color called Tayberry Jam. The deep gold of Evening Lanternglow. The pink of May Peony. But we settled on the closest match we could find to the shadow of the old paint, Windward-Alee Blue.

I follow the shadow of the old letters, outlining them with a thin brush, and then filling them in. I stay, going over the shapes again, waiting for the letters to dry. I stay with this point on the earth that showed me my name.

# BASTIÁN

efore I leave Antonio's, I slip alebrijes into the pantry and into his jacket pockets. When I get home, I put some next to the laundry soap, and in with the oranges, to see how long it'll take Mom and Mamá to notice.

When I leave foxes in Lore's room, they find them almost instantly. But instead of saying something, they put one back in my room, one in my bag. I'm guessing a couple will show up in my locker when school starts.

This is one way I talk to the world, in the purple of mallow flowers, the green of milk thistle leaves, the orange of the tiny pumpkins Mamá puts on our windowsills in fall. These are things I can say with my hands.

My ADHD is made out of paradoxes and contradictions. It's having weirdly high energy and then getting tapped out fast. It's making impulsive decisions and then being unable to make them at all. It's inattention and hyperfocus. It's being so sensitive I can feel everything around me and being so oblivious I miss things that seem obvious. It's acting too fast, and being too slow. It's thinking everything is possible and then wondering if anything is possible for me.

My brain is a shifting landscape. It will always have light and shadow and color, but the shapes and shades will change. So I try to claim all of myself, wherever I am in the seiches that move through my brain. It's the only way I can break out of thinking that I am only as good as the last thing I've done, or as the weather inside my brain. It's the only way I get out from under the lie that good days mean I'm worthy and bad days mean I'm irretrievably lost.

I used to think the only options were the world under the lake and the world above it, good moments in my brain and bad moments in my brain, parts of me worth keeping and parts worth forgetting. But maybe that makes as little sense as thinking there's only *boy* and *girl* and nothing in between. I'm proof of what exists between, and so is Lore, and everyone like us, just like the world under the lake is proof that there's something between air and water.

When Lore and I go to the inlet, silver-green leaves lift off the edge of the lake. The lapping against the rocks turns to slate-blue wings.

We don't wait for the world under the lake to find us. We come here, and we find it first.

Lore and I may be constantly mapping the landscapes of our own brains. But the raw beauty in us, it's something living and breathing. It's no more real or true above the surface or below it, but this is where we remind each other and ourselves of what we already know.

We don't have to be unafraid of our own hearts to be proud of everything they hold.

"You ready?" Lore asks.

I nod.

The sky around us darkens, and a familiar, faint glow shows up under our feet. The whole ground brightens and dims in patches of green and milk blue and amber.

We go forward.

To the rest of the world, we vanish.

But to each other, we're seen.

# AUTHOR'S NOTE

Bastián's story is one portrayal of living with ADHD (attention deficit hyperactivity disorder), and Lore's is one portrayal of living with dyslexia. I am not a doctor or a mental health care professional, and none of what I've written in this book is intended as professional advice. I write from my lived experience, and from my own neuro-divergent brain, like I write from my lived experience being nonbinary and Mexican American.

In some ways, I am exactly what some people think of when they think of ADHD. Friends joke about how I run outside when it's hailing. How I will completely lose my train of thought at the sight of a cat or a butterfly. How I can sometimes be so high energy I'm vibrating with it.

But those close to me have also seen the other side of my ADHD. They've seen me burn myself out trying to hide what's going on in my own brain, which I didn't understand until a doctor saw a pattern in what, to me, had previously felt random.

I'm deeply grateful to the doctors who diagnosed my ADHD and dyslexia. It illuminated a childhood of making myself sit still in class, and then getting into fights on the playground. Of forcing myself to seem as normal as possible, and then collapsing in on myself. Of knowing I needed to not be too loud or too conspicuous, because as a child of color, I had little margin for error.

Sometimes my ADHD is hard to separate out from my dyslexia. They both exist in my brain at the same time, and have some overlapping effects. My experiences with dyslexia led to impulse-control-draining frustration, and worsened conflicts with teachers and peers.

But here's where I got lucky: Like Lore, I have a mother who's all the proof I needed that just because our brains work differently doesn't mean we're stupid. My mother graduated from high school without knowing how to read. If you think you have to be incredibly smart to manage that, you're right.

Both my mother and my father read out loud to me, and both these things were acts of love—on my mother's part because, after learning to read in her twenties, she still stumbled over words, and on my father's part because he could barely get through a paragraph without me asking questions.

I learned to read because a few very patient family members, like my mother and my father, and a few very patient teachers and librarians, read with me. I memorized words by the sounds of their voices and their hands pointing to what line they were on. That was my access point to language, the patience and openness of the adults in my life who did not let me fall through the cracks in a system that would call me troubled, or obstinate, or unreachable before it would ever call me a reader.

I learned to read because of the people who decided I was curious instead of stupid and stubborn, that my brain was wired a little differently instead of wired wrong.

That lesson, that different wasn't wrong, was one I had to learn about my own gender identity. That existing as who I truly am is as valid as reading the way I realistically can.

Those of us who are transgender and nonbinary, we are beautiful.

Those of us whose brains don't process language or don't process the world in the way we're often told we should, we are brilliant.

Before we part ways for now, reader, I have a favor to ask: If you can read to and with the children in your life, please do. If you can encourage others to read to and with the children in their lives, please do. No matter how a child's brain is wired, no matter how they experience the world around them, they likely won't think the world of books is theirs too unless someone invites them into it. Those we trust show us the path into stories.

If no one had read to me, I wouldn't have learned to read.

If no one had read to me, I wouldn't be writing these words.

To every one of you who does for someone else what my family and community did for me, thank you.

# RESOURCES

To learn more about ADHD, dyslexia, and gender identity:

**CHADD**

chadd.org

**ADDitude**

additudemag.com

**INTERNATIONAL DYSLEXIA ASSOCIATION**

dyslexiaida.org

**NATIONAL CENTER FOR LEARNING DISABILITIES**

ncld.org

**GENDER SPECTRUM**

genderspectrum.org

# ACKNOWLEDGMENTS

My heart feels like a glitter jar when I think about everyone who was part of this story becoming a book. I'm grateful for every one of them. I'll name a few here:

The doctors and mental health professionals who diagnosed my ADHD and my dyslexia, and who help me navigate the work of living the best life I can with the brain I've got.

Kat Brzozowski, for being both a spectacularly brilliant editor and a fearless ally.

Jean Feiwel, for making Bastián, Lore, and me part of the Feiwel & Friends family.

Brittany Pearlman, for helping my books make their way in the world (and for calling me an enby-friendly nickname before I even came out).

Rich Deas, for the amazing art direction at MacKids;

Liz Dresner, for your stunning vision for this book and for putting two trans characters on the cover; Carolina Rodriguez Fuenmayor, for your absolutely incredible art.

Pat McHugh, Jessica White, Dawn Ryan, Celeste Cass, and Ilana Worrell, and really, let me say thank you again to all the editors, copy editors, managing editors, production managers, and production team members who've worked on my books, because working with a dyslexic author can make this rigorous work even more challenging, and your patience and graciousness is a gift.

Everyone at Feiwel & Friends and Macmillan Children's Publishing Group: Emily Settle, Liz Szabla, Erin Siu, Teresa Ferraiolo, Kim Waymer, Jon Yaged, Allison Verost, Molly Ellis, Leigh Ann Higgins, Cynthia Lliguichuzhca, Allegra Green, Jo Kirby, Kathryn Little, Julia Gardiner, Lauren Scobell, Alexei Esikoff, Mariel Dawson, Avia Perez, Dominique Jenkins, Meg Collins, Gabriella Salpeter, Romanie Rout, Ebony Lane, Kristin Dulaney, Jordan Winch, Kaitlin Loss, Rachel Diebel, Foyinsi Adegbonmire, Amanda Barillas, Morgan Dubin, Morgan Rath, Madison Furr, Mary Van Akin, Kelsey Marrujo, Holly West, Anna Roberto, Katie Quinn, Hana Tzou; Katie Halata, Lucy Del Priore, Melissa Croce, Kristen Luby, and Cierra Bland of Macmillan School & Library; and the many more who turn stories into books and help readers find them.

Nova Ren Suma, Emily X.R. Pan, Anica Mrose Rissi, Aisha Saeed, Emery Lord, Dahlia Adler, Elana K. Arnold,

Sara Ryan, Cory McCarthy, A.S. King, and all the writer friends I've written with, brainstormed with, and shared spaces with, both physical and virtual, while writing this book.

E.K. Johnston, Emma Higinbotham, Chandra Rooney, Lindsay Smith, F.M. Boughan, Tara Sim, and Molly Owen, who held space for me alongside a lake when I was a newly out enby, and whose creative energy was there when lake magic first took over my brain.

Lindsay Eagar, Lee O'Brien, and Karen McCoy for helping me go deeper into these characters and their worlds.

Taylor Martindale Kean, Stefanie Sanchez Von Borstel, and the Full Circle Literary team, and Taryn Fagerness and the Taryn Fagerness Agency, for your advocacy for stories and their authors.

My mother and father, for listening to the passages I wrote on dyslexia, and for helping my dyslexic brain learn how to read in the first place.

My fellow neurodivergent brains, and my fellow trans and nonbinary siblings—I am so grateful for the communities we make together.

Readers, for bringing stories to life in your hearts. Thank you.